THE MAUI MURDERS

Also by Marty Martins

The Blizzard

The Yellow Balloon

~~

THE MAUI MURDERS

Death and Romance on the Valley Isle

MARTY MARTINS

MANŌ PAʻELE
PUBLISHING

The Maui Murders: Death and Romance on the Valley Isle

Manō Paʻele Publishing
PO Box 1485
Kīhei, HI 96753

ISBNs:
978-0-9845680-9-3 (softcover)
978-0-9845680-8-6 (eBook)

Cover design by Reese Dante. reesedante.com

Printed in the United States of America

10 9 8 7 6 5 4 3 2

To Kyle
Koʻu kaikunāne mai kekahi makuahine.

THE MAUI MURDERS

Death and Romance on the Valley Isle

ACKNOWLEDGMENTS

Writing a novel requires research if it is to sound authentic. There is only so much one can do online or at the library. I was fortunate to have two former law-enforcement colleagues more than willing to give me the benefit of their knowledge.

First, a *mahalo* to San Diego Sheriff's **Detective Nancy Ryan** for info on SDSO hierarchy and standard department firearms.

Next, thank you to retired **Detective Sergeant Paul Conway** of the San Diego Police Department's Homicide Team 4 and later their Cold Case Unit. Paul read the entire manuscript and made important contributions on homicide-investigation methods and on police procedures.

Retired Maui Deputy Chief of Police **Kekūhaupiʻo "Keku" Akana** was *wikiwiki nui* with a reply when I had a last-minute question about department equipment.

Many thanks to my former classmate **Makalani Franco-Francis** for her kōkua on my hula questions. Maka, with her hālau, is a veteran of five consecutive Merrie Monarch competitions (the Super Bowl of hula), including one all-around world championship. She is still an active dancer and assistant instructor.

Mahalo to **Kumu Kui Gapero**, who is ever patient with my spur-of-the-moment ʻōlelo Hawaiʻi questions.

Dr. Linda Tetor, a local physician and fellow outrigger-canoe paddler, is always generous with her time and knowledge when I have a medical question. Thank you again, Doc.

Thank you to **Brett Collett**, a firefighter at MauiFire Station 14, for explaining the proper names and functions of equipment on a fire engine.

Mahalo nui to **Ronald C. Williams, PhD**, historian and former archivist at the Hawai'i State Archives, for his quick help confirming my speculation on an historical issue.

I believe it is almost impossible for an author to proofread and neutrally judge one's own work. It's my good fortune to have trusted friends willing to give me their time.

Thanks, again, to **Rebecca Ocain, Esq.,** my attorney, former colleague, and BFF, for her proofreading skill and her always-helpful and incisive comments and suggestions, all of which were adopted.

I'm also thankful for the encouragement and cogent—and seriouly considered—suggestions from fellow author **Cris Hoover.**

A big hat tip to **Frank Kresen**, my editor, and Project Manager **Ronda Rawlins** at 1106 Design.

Steve Casey, journalist, editor, raconteur, is always there when I need him. Thanks, my friend.

The map on page 2 was provided by **Rachael Lallo** of Brandcrafters. Much appreciated!

AUTHOR'S NOTES

This is a work of fiction. There are real places and businesses used to set scenes, but all the characters, situations, and dialogue are entirely from my imagination. If any of those resemble, sound like, or appear to be someone or something you've seen or heard, it is entirely coincidental.

While it is true Maui County hired a new police chief from Nevada a while back, my fictional police chief came from San Diego because I needed a device to get my protagonist from California to Maui. Also, the National Park Police and Maui PD cannot go car-to-car on their radios (maybe someday they will), the parking garage at the real mall is smaller and not configured like the made-up one in the story, and Lia's personalized license plate is fake (too many letters). The decree by King Kamehameha III that the heroine relies on in Chapter One has been debunked as fraudulent, but she doesn't know that, and her reliance on it advances the story. That's why it's called fiction.

Although this story involves a fictionalized version of the Maui Police Department, it is *not* about Maui PD. Nothing in the story is intended to embarrass the department or its officers; I apologize in advance if any offense, even inadvertently, is given. Being retired law enforcement myself, not to mention the son of a 30-year police veteran, I have the highest respect for police officers and what they do. All the Maui police officers I have interacted with have been highly professional, despite being understaffed (down more than 145 officers) and underpaid (17% below the national average).

You will notice this novel is peppered with Hawaiian words and even full sentences.

Hawai'i is the only "state" with two official languages: 'Ōlelo Hawai'i (Hawaiian) and English. So, it seems only appropriate that a novel set in Hawai'i should have some native lingo. If the translation is not provided nearby or cannot be deduced from the context, there's always Google Translate or the Hawaiian-English dictionary (https://hilo. hawaii.edu/wehe/).

And, as if there was any doubt, I am not Hawaiian. I have the highest respect for the Hawaiian people, their culture, and rich history, and am proud to be an immigrant to this storied island nation.

PROLOGUE

DEL KURTZ put himself away and pulled up his zipper. He looked down at the woman lying in apparent repose, her hands over her face, her legs still spread.

Who knew sex could be such a thrill.

✦ ✦ ✦

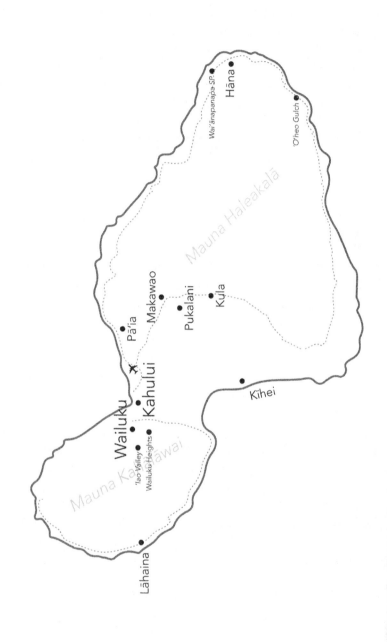

CHAPTER 1

THE PRE-DAWN SKY was just beginning to lighten when Lia Reynolds released the straps holding her board to the truck rack. She was parked on the shoulder, tight up against the trees and foliage. As always, she pulled off the road before, or sometimes after, the big hau tree with its mass of tangled branches and the barely perceptible hole in the large 'ulei bushes. She was happy to see that the African tulip tree that had been girdled by one of Auntie Carol's sons or grandsons was doing a nice job of dying. The highly invasive species could grow six feet a day and, while its bright orange flowers looked nice, the tree's tall canopy cut off the light and killed native plants and trees below it.

Taking one more look in both directions to ensure no cars, joggers, or dog walkers were in sight, she tucked the board under her left arm and ducked into the woods. There was no path, but she had cut through these trees so many times, she recognized them as signposts, telling her when to carry the board vertically to make the next turn, when to bow down under that low branch on the false sandalwood, when to pirouette around the thorny kiawe that always tried to attack her. And then she came out at *her* beach and a small cove she had discovered by accident when driven mauka by a sudden squall. A hundred feet to her left rose a high, black cliff. It couldn't be seen from down here, but some Canadian billionaire's mansion sat on top of it somewhere. If she turned slightly to her left, straight ahead was the island of Kahoʻolawe, seven miles away. Between here and there was the tiny, crescent-shaped islet of Molokini. Down the beach to her right, the shore was rock under jagged lava that came down from the woods, a reminder of the dormant volcano's last eruption in the 1790s. She knew it was a miracle that greedy developers hadn't already carved it into mini-estates for wealthy, part-time residents from North America.

But here, about half the length of a football field, was an off-white beach, thanks to generations of uhu, parrotfish, and other coral-eating sea creatures each pooping out a pound or more of sand every year.

Lia set her board, a CJ Nelson Apex, on the sand and ran her hand over the top, feeling for any spots that needed coverage. She took the bar of body-warmed wax from her pocket, peeled back the wrapper, and touched up the surface where it was needed. The sky was brighter now, the degree of lighting the wedding photographers liked at the tourist beaches. Dawn had occurred more than 30 minutes earlier, but the sun still hadn't gotten over the 10,000-plus feet of Mauna Haleakalā. High enough, though, that she could see where the turquoise of the near-shore kai turned into the dark blue of the moana and the pink on the far-horizon clouds.

Lia kicked off her slippers, unbuttoned and unzipped her jean cutoffs and let them drop to her feet, pulled the tank top off over her head, and then picked up her board and ran into the water. Even though the ocean was warmer than the morning's ambient temperature, she experienced the usual shock of her skin adjusting to the sea. She had to paddle out some distance, past the end of the cliff, to reach the breaking waves, and today the sets were coming in at a steady pace.

A small one was coming behind her as soon as she got past the point, so she popped up for a warm-up run. She dropped back onto the board as soon as the wave petered out and began the long paddle back out to where the waves were building. The paddling out always took two or three times the length of an actual ride, but it was good exercise, too.

The sets were coming in pretty steadily, and the waves were holding their shape long enough that she started counting how many bottom turns she could get out of each face.

The sun was higher, and the wind was picking up. She saw a huge wave building and got in position just in time to catch it. *This is the kind you live for*, she thought. The power of the water was driving her forward; the ehu kai, the spray off the top of the wave, was hitting her in the back. She walked to the front of the board, saw she had enough ocean left, and dropped her toes over the front lip of her board, letting the power of tons of water counterbalance her. When she felt the wave start to weaken, she walked backwards and carved the board toward the beach, finally forced to paddle back to the shore. It was her 12th run of the morning, and she chose to quit on a high note.

When it got shallow enough so that she could stand up, she lifted her board under her arm and was walking out of the water when she saw a guy on the beach staring at her. *Ogling* was more like it. He was young, tan, definitely in good shape, and wearing brown board shorts with yellow and orange trim. As she got closer and could make out his facial features, she decided he was all or a large part kanaka maoli and that his dark skin wasn't from a tan.

"Showing off out there, huh?"

Who was this guy, and who made him a surfing judge?

"It's only showing off if you know someone is watching, and I had no idea you picked my beach to watch from."

"*Your* beach? Actually, it's my beach."

"There are no private beaches in Hawai'i ," she retorted.

"So you admit it's not *your* beach?"

She couldn't help but pick up on the sarcasm in his voice. On normal days, she would just lie on her board until she was dry before getting dressed. Today, she turned her back to him, pulled on her tank top, untied the neck and back knots on her bikini top, and pulled it out under her tank before putting on her shorts over her wet suit.

"I see the board shorts, but where's your board?"

"On my car."

"So if you agree there are no private beaches in Hawai'i, how could this be *your* beach?" she asked, glancing sideways at him while she picked up her board.

"Well, that woods you're about to cut through *is* private property, and it belongs to my family."

"Ha! I know the family who owns it, and I have Auntie Carol's permission to cut through." *Will this guy ever leave me alone?*

"Is that right? So you know my tūtū?"

"If she's your tūtū, I guess I do. Are you an Opio or some other branch?"

"Justin Opio. What's your name?"

"Lia Reynolds."

"You surf pretty good, Lia Reynolds, so I guess you're not a tourist."

She exhaled a huff. "I'm a kama'āina," pride evident in her tone.

"Oh, so you've lived here long enough to get a discount at the ABC store?"

She was tempted to say "Fuck you," but she told herself "kapu aloha" and bit her tongue. "ABC doesn't give a kamaʻāina discount, but why do I think you already knew that?

"No, I'm a native Hawaiian."

"*You're* a native Hawaiian?"

"Yes. You *do* know what 'kamaʻāina' really means, don't you?" she said in a tone like she was speaking to a child. "I was born here, so yes, I'm a native Hawaiian."

Justin could tell this argument wasn't going anywhere, but he didn't want her to leave. "You're awful white for native Hawaiian, despite the great tan."

"Scotch-Irish and Portuguese with a little English, Chinese, and Dutch in there somewhere, not that skin color has anything to do with it."

"So then how can you call yourself a native Hawaiian?"

Lia dropped her board and threw up her hands. "Oh, my God! How many times do I have to say it? I was born here! I'm a native Hawaiian! You *do* know the difference between a native Hawaiian and a kanaka maoli, I hope?

"You look like a kanaka. If you are, lucky you. If you were born here, you are *also* a native Hawaiian. Got it?"

"Who told you that you being born here made you a native Hawaiian?"

Lia rolled her eyes. "Kauikeauoli, for one."

"Who's that?"

"I don't have time for this," she replied, expelling a breath in frustration. "Study your own history, or take the easy way and ask your tūtū." With that, she picked up her board and disappeared into the woods.

+ + +

CHAPTER 2

TWO WEEKS EARLIER

DEL KURTZ had been laid off from his janitorial job more than a month ago. He hadn't been able to find a job that paid enough to cover his food, rent, and expenses, which included his iPhone and his about-to-expire monthly bus pass. Yesterday, he had come home from job-hunting to find a notice taped to the door of his tiny studio apartment. He had five days to pay his overdue rent or be evicted.

While scrolling through Facebook—his FB name was Kerl Denuts, a takeoff on his real names but allowing him anonymity from any personnel managers and HR flunkies who went searching for social-media dirt on him—he saw an ad for a sale at Southwest Airlines with a one-way fare to Hawai'i. *What the hell? I've always wanted to go to Hawai'i. I'll find a job there.*

He bought a ticket using his neighbor's credit card on the last day of the sale and paid him back with a part of the cash he had emptied from his credit-union account that morning. He learned online that Southwest would let him sit anywhere he wanted, depending on when he checked in, but he couldn't do that until 24 hours before takeoff.

He gave away his small appliances and other items worth anything to people who were friendly to him in his building. He neatly folded and packed a clean pair of jeans and camouflage cargo pants, a clean polo shirt and five

T-shirts, a swimming suit, eight pairs of rolled-up socks, his toiletries, and his phone-charging cord. His jacket was attached to the outside of the backpack with the straps. He kept out a set of clean clothes for the flight. On the way into the bathroom, his green/brown hazel eyes looked at himself in the mirror. His five-foot, eight-inch, medium frame was lean and strong. He ran his fingers through his longish brown hair and wished he had gotten a haircut before the trip.

He showered, shaved, and slept naked the night before his departure, was up before dawn, ate breakfast at the neighborhood McDonald's, and took the bus to Oakland International Airport. Before he got off, he handed his bus pass to a man whose dirty hair, gray whiskers, and grimy clothes strongly suggested the old-timer was homeless. "It has five days left. Good luck," he told him and got off feeling good about himself.

As he sat in the waiting area outside his boarding gate, he did some girl-watching and wondered about the women in Hawai'i. Finally, boarding was announced. He was excited about this new adventure. He was number A16 in the first boarding group. He walked down the jetway to the plane, stowed his bag, and sat in the emergency-exit row because of the extra leg room.

Del hadn't been on a plane since he was a teenager on a trip to visit his grandmother for the summer, so he was disappointed to learn they did not serve any meals. He heard the announcement for some overpriced snacks for sale and settled for a small bag of complimentary pretzels and a package of blueberry breakfast biscuits washed down with a can of tomato juice because it was more filling than orange or cranberry juice. Later, when he went to use the bathroom adjacent to the rear galley, he saw the basket of snack items sitting on the counter. He apologized for interrupting the two flight attendants, who were sitting and having an obviously non-work-related conversation, and asked if he could please have another snack, and the friendly FA said, "Help yourself." So he took a big handful and shoved them in his pocket.

The plane got to Maui just before noon. Del had forgotten that it took some time for the plane to taxi and park after it landed. He felt the big jet finally come to a sudden stop. After a short delay, a chime sounded. The other passengers obviously knew what it meant because they all stood up, so he stood up, too. He retrieved his bag from the overhead compartment and set it on the seat while he waited for everyone ahead of the emergency exit to walk forward to deplane.

He just followed the crowd, and when he saw the overhead sign for Baggage Claim/Parking, he knew where they were going. Having only a carry-on item, he continued on, followed the mob down an escalator, passed the luggage carousels, and headed toward the doors.

Once out on the sidewalk, he wondered what to do next. *So this is what Hawai'i looks like.* It was sunny and warm, with a hot wind blowing, making the tops of the palm trees sway. A group of older people with some kind of tour were boarding a shuttle bus to a place called Ka'anapali, so he started chatting with a couple and just got on as if he were part of the group.

He shuffled through the stack of free brochures he had picked up from a rack on his way out of the airport and found a map. Ka'anapali was somewhere up the west side of the island, and, between the smaller inset map and two other brochures, he learned that Ka'anapali was just a string of expensive, high-rise resort hotels along a big beach north of a town called Lāhainā.

He enjoyed the scenic trip along the coast, looking at all the water and across to other islands. It seemed a lot different from the ocean in California. The bus went through a tunnel, and there were cliffs covered with metal netting, he assumed to prevent rockslides. Farther on, he saw people riding on surfboards for the first time in real life. The waves were much smaller, though, than the ones he'd seen on TV or movies.

Further north, the road moved away from the coast and went up a grade that provided an even better view. His map told him this was the Lāhainā bypass. He wanted to get off in Lāhainā and not go past it! Luckily, the bus came off the bypass road back into town and had to stop for a red light. Del grabbed his backpack and ran to the front of the bus, demanding to get off. The driver said he was not allowed to let passengers off here. Del leaned over close to the driver's face and, in a man-to-man private conversation, told him he was about to have the runs and unless he wanted a passenger with shit running down his leg onto the floor, he'd better hurry and open the door. The driver complied, thanking his lucky stars. He thought he actually smelled the guy starting to have bowel trouble.

It was early afternoon and quite hot. He had a 12-inch sandwich and large water at Subway for lunch and spent the day just strolling through the town, going in and out of all the little shops, almost all geared toward tourists. Del saw that most of the local people and many of the tourists were wearing flip-flops. His high-top shoes were really hot, and he'd have to change socks when he found a quiet place to sit down. Occasionally, a cool breeze would blow in off the nearby water, and he felt the temperature slowly starting to drop by the middle of the afternoon.

There were restaurants, a lot of them fish places, up and down the main drag, which he learned was Front Street. A look at the menus posted outside many of them indicated their meals were outside the range of his limited budget. He'd have to be frugal until he found a job.

He did see the largest banyan tree in the United States, and there was no fee to tour the Old Lāhainā Courthouse and Customs House. There was a museum on the second floor. On the way out, he put a dollar in the donation box.

He walked to the harbor, sat on the wall, and watched boats coming in for the evening. Two others were boarding passengers for sunset dinner cruises. He stayed to watch the sunset. His phone said it was near 7:00 p.m.. But he didn't get to watch the sun sink into the ocean because there was another island in the way. He went to a different Subway close to where he was, because he knew he could afford anything on their menu, plus he had a coupon on the back of his receipt from lunch for a free drink with a 12-inch sandwich and chips, so that's what he got—except the meatball sandwich rather than the ham and cheese he'd had earlier. He took his time eating so he could hang out there until they closed for the night at nine.

Del didn't know what he was going to do for the night. It was getting cold, so he put on his jacket and sat on a park bench to rest and changed socks while he was there. He must have dozed off, because, when he woke up, it was nearly eleven. He had to remind himself, it was one in the morning, California time, and he had gotten up super early to make his 5:00 a.m. flight. He started north on Front Street, looking for a place to sleep.

HIS INSTINCT HAD been to run, but Del Kurtz knew it was likely to attact attention. Instead, he had pulled his cap lower on his forehead and casually walked away. His first thought was to get out of this shopping-complex parking lot. He was sure there must be security cameras. He cut west to Front Street, which was well lit, although all the shops were closed, but chatter or music still spilled from a few restaurants and bars. He turned left at the next corner and soon saw a McDonald's farther down the street. It would be a good place to sit down for a little bit.

He took the tray with the Big Mac and a large coffee, and found the table farthest from the door but was unsure if he would make it. Suddenly, his whole body was jittery. Delayed reaction, he guessed. He sat down, popped the lid off the coffee, sipped some of the boiling-hot liquid, and replayed the entire night in his mind.

She didn't have to be so nasty. He had seen her squat to piss in a dark alleyway. He made her out as a prostitute right away by the immodest outfit and excessive makeup. He couldn't tell one Asian from another. She could be Japanese, Korean, or Filipino, he guessed. All he knew for sure was she had slanty eyes. When he first approached her, he figured she mistook him as a potential customer. All he did was ask her about a place to *sleep*. Sleep, not go to bed! There was no reason her for to raise her voice, getting so shrill, belittling him, saying *she worked for her money, who did he think he was, anyway*, and so on.

He had lost his temper and slapped her across the face. Then she started screaming at the top of her lungs like she was being murdered. In afterthought, he laughed about the irony of that. He had gotten his hands around her neck just to shut her up as he walked her backwards into that alley. The more she fought, the tighter he squeezed. Then, suddenly, she went limp. It excited him now to think about it. Watching her eyes roll back in her head with her tongue sticking out. *You work for your money, you little bitch? Well, how about one on the house?* he had asked the lifeless woman. When they were deep in the shadows of the alley, he had jerked off her panties, pulling off both high-heeled shoes in the process, and drove himself into her repeatedly, so hard he thought he'd bruised his dick. Coming was almost anti-climactic after the high of his hands around her neck and watching her go limp. He was getting a woody right now just thinking about it. The cash, almost $180 in her purse, and a cell phone were nice bonuses, too.

Smiling, he devoured his burger and coffee. While he ate, he turned on her phone. *What? No password? Stupid.* He scrolled through the photos on her phone. Sure enough, he found a number of nude and topless selfies. He didn't think anyone saw to call the cops but decided he'd better move on.

As he left the restaurant, he looked up and looked directly into a security camera. *Fuck!* Then he remembered that it was possible to track the movements of a smartphone. Better play it safe. He started walking south from the restaurant. He pulled off the glittery pink case, threw it in the gutter, and used his pocket knife to pry open the phone. After removing the battery and the chip, he dropped them in the sewer. A half-block later, he threw the phone parts into two different yards. He didn't need hers anyway—he had his own.

There was a church up ahead with some spotlights on the façade and a statue with flowers. He saw a bus at the stop sign with its blinker on. He expanded his view and saw the sign for the bus stop nearby. He had to run to catch it.

THE BUS ROUTE ended at Queen Kaʻahumanu Center, a two-story shopping mall. The mall was closed, and he needed a place to sleep. Rooms were so expensive here, Del had learned from searching on his phone during the bus ride. The fact was he couldn't afford even one night at a shitty hotel, assuming one even existed. He wandered out the back of the mall into the multi-level parking garage. He saw a bag lady setting up camp across the way under some stairs.

After checking each level for possible places to sleep, he returned to the bottom deck and saw a faded green Datsun pickup with a camper shell backed in against the wall in the corner opposite the stairwell, where the woman and her shopping cart of junk were. Through the dust-covered windshield, he could see a placard with the mall logo and the words "Permitted Overnight Parking."

Hell, I wonder how long this thing has been here. He tried the doors, which were locked, and then went around the back. He had to squeeze in to reach the handle on the camper shell, gave it a twist, and it opened! *Probably why the guy backed in against the wall.* There was room to open the camper door but not enough room to fully lower the tailgate. He had to slither against the wall to get his right foot on the bumper. With his back braced against the wall, he got the other foot on the bumper, moved the right foot into the camper, pushed his backpack inside, and gingerly slid his body sideways against the wall until he could lower himself into the camper. Once turned around, he pulled the tailgate closed and reached out to lower the camper door. As he did so, he looked around to see if anyone was looking. Sure enough, that old hag was sitting under the stairwell, watching the whole thing. *Ha! Probably jealous she hadn't thought of it first, not that she could have squirmed her way in like I did.*

Once his eyes adjusted to the darkness, Del saw it was better than expected. At the front of the camper, a narrow sheet of plywood rested on three sides of the pickup box, covered with a ratty piece of thick foam rubber, and a sleeping bag. Well, it wasn't the Marriott, but it was free.

He also discovered there was a crawl-through between the camper and the cab of the truck. The windows in each had been removed and some sort of donut thing inserted between them, to keep out rain and debris, he assumed.

It was too warm to use the sleeping bag, so after he took off his shoes, pants, and shirt, he slept on top of it, but not before setting the alarm clock on his phone.

✦ ✦ ✦

CHAPTER 3

"CAN YOU BELIEVE THAT?" Lia Reynolds said, her tone incredulous.

"Since when did you mind having a guy check you out?" replied her friend Miki'ala Kanae, across the table at the Akamai Coffee shop.

"Yeah, check me out like a once-over, but this guy was watching me all the way into the beach. I mean *staring*!"

"What were you wearing?"

"You remember that blue bikini I bought when we were at that Kai Piha store at Wailea Shops?"answered Lia after blowing on her mocha latte with two pumps of caramel.

"You mean those three little triangles and some skinny string, including the one running between your butt cheeks?!"

"Yeah, that one, but I never wear it in public—just at that deserted cove where I surf. It's kinda sexy, sorta like surfing naked."

"No wonder the guy was staring!" Miki'ala held the straw as she took a drink of her iced coffee and then put the cup down. "Was he some old lech?"

"No. I thought I said, he was our age. And a kanaka, which I thought made it even more rude."

"Native guys don't check out girls?" asked Miki'ala, her tone implying disbelief.

"Well, of course, they do, but not staring like that guy. It felt creepy. And then we got into this argument about the difference between a native Hawaiian and kanaka maoli."

"So, tell me: besides being a kanaka, what did he look like? Already getting a beer belly?"

"Hardly. A bronze, buff BP. Six-pack, short hair, and brown eyes, of course. And taller than me."

Miki'ala laughed out loud. "And who was checking out who?"

"I told you—*checking out* is like a quick once-over to get the picture, not a frickin' *medical exam*. I didn't *stare*."

"Though you would've liked to?"

"Shut up."

Lia took a gulp of her coffee and spit most of it back in the cup. "Damn, still too hot."

"When do you start work?" asked Miki'ala.

Both their phones were on the table, and Lia tapped her screen. "About ten more minutes. I can hardly be late 'cause the manager will start giving me the stink eye in five."

Miki'ala chuckled, having received enough of them in her own life.

"Oh, shit—there he is now!"

"Your manager?"

"No, the guy! Don't look! He's coming right this way."

Miki'ala swung her head around toward the door, and Lia's eyes rolled up into her head. Miki'ala grinned, stood up, said, "Kekoa!" and was met with a traditional hug and cheek kiss that she returned.

"Miki'ala! So good to see you! How long has it been?"

"So long I'm surprised you remember me."

"How could I forget the girl who beat me in the fourth-grade spelling contest?" They both laughed.

"Is that all you remember?" she teased.

"Of course not. I have some blurry memories from high school, too."

She laughed, recalling the same steamy memories. "Is that why you changed schools halfway through junior year never to be seen again until now?" she teased.

"What can I say? You ruined me. Nahh, I moved to California with the family."

Then, turning to Lia, he said, "Aloha hou." Unsure of her knowledge of ʻōlelo Hawaiʻi, he added, "That means..."

"I know what 'Hello again' means," she said as she stood up, her tone condescending.

"Oh, sorry," he said, grinning, but happy to get a close-up view of the tall blonde.

"So, Kekoa, I hear you've already met my friend, Lia."

"Indeed, I have. A short but pleasant meeting," he smirked, but really noticing for the first time how tall she was.

Lia gritted her teeth, eyes squinting.

"Join us," invited Mikiʻala.

Oh great, thought Lia.

"Mahalo, but no. I called in an order and just ran in to pick it up. Probably cold by now," he kidded.

It would serve you right for bothering us.

The drinks were waiting at the counter, and he stopped to give each woman an awkward hug and cheek buss without spilling any coffee from the cups in the cardboard tray. "Good seeing you, Mikiʻala." Then, after a tiny pause, "Hope to see you again, too, Lia."

"Yeah, Justin," Lia replied, intentionally using the name he had provided her.

They were both watching him go out the door when Lia's manager said, "Lia, didn't your shift start two minutes ago?"

"Just conducting some customer relations on my own time, Ralph. Doing my small part to promote Akamai Coffee."

"*Justin*?" queried Miki'ala.

"That was the only name he gave me.

"So what did he mean about 'blurry memories' and you 'ruined' him? Did you do him?"

"Maybe I should have," she teased suggestively. "No, just some minor petting after Winter Formal. It was a Catholic school, after all."

Lia pressed cheeks with Miki'ala and said, "I hafta go. Class tonight. You're still picking me up, right?"

"Hiki nō. Be ready!"

THE NOON RUSH was over, and Lia was wiping the wall shelves, her back to the door.

"Kamehameha the Third," announced a male voice behind her.

Lia turned around and saw it was that friend of Miki'ala's from yesterday. *What was his name? Oh, yeah, Justin aka Kekoa.*

She held up both hands, palms up, one still holding the towel, lifted her chin a quarter inch and exhaled audibly through her nose. "OK, I'll bite. What about him?"

"No. Kauikeauoli!"

"Yeah, I know that was his name." Suddenly remembering their conversation on the beach, "Ohh, you've been doing some homework, huh, island boy? Who did you ask, your grandma?"

"Wikipedia."

Lia snorted, shaking her head with a grin. "So, is that all you came in to tell me, or are you going to order something?"

"Are you here by yourself?"

"My shift partner is on break—why?"

"Is that the manager?"

"No, I'm the on-duty manager. You're lucky it's slow right now, because you sure ask a lot of questions for a non-paying customer." She had to admit she was enjoying the repartee, and the guy *was* a hunk.

"OK, listen. Can we start again?"

"From Kamehameha the Third or from when you were undressing me with your eyes yesterday?"

"Well, you have to admit, there wasn't a lot left for my eyes to do."

Lia blushed but smirked. "OK, from today. Hold on. I have some *paying* customers."

When she came back, she cheerily said, "Aloha awakea. What can I get for you, sir?"

"Aloha nō. Small black coffee—" He leaned over as if to get a better look at her name tag, and added, "Lia." While she turned to pour the coffee, he introduced himself. "My name is Kekoa Opio."

"Nice to meet you, Kekoa."

"Did you go out this morning?"

"I did. Walked through your tūtū's woods and had the *public* beach all to myself." She heard his chuckle before she continued, "Did you know that beach disappears in the winter? All the sand washes out."

"Yes, or at least it did when I was a kid, but it always comes back in the spring."

He was opening up his wallet, and she said, "That's OK—it's on the house." But before he could flip it closed, she saw what looked like a metal star inside. She reached out and put her hand on his wrist, both of them instantly aware of the physical contact.

"What is that? Are you a cop or something?"

"Deputy sheriff. In California. San Diego County."

Lia nodded, acknowledging that she was impressed. "Can I see it?"

He flipped the wallet open again and displayed the silver badge that was inset in the leather. "It's what we call a 'flat badge.' Not like the kind you wear on a uniform."

"Is that why you're always asking so many questions? It's just a cop habit?"

"Deputy sheriff. In California, the police are cops. But you're right, *cop* is kind of a general term for local law-enforcement officers. Sheriffs in America are different from the ones here, and they have a lot more power."

Lia nodded her understanding as she wiped off the counter to look busy.

"Are you going out tomorrow?" he asked.

"Probably. It looks like this high surf will last, but I'll check the reports tonight."

"Mind some company?"

"If you think you can handle it. From your talk with Miki, it sounds like you've been away for a while."

"They *do* surf in California."

"OK. We'll see. I get there early."

"MAKA, SUPPER IS in the crockpot," said Celeste Ohukai D'Sousa before she left to start her shift as a pediatric surgical nurse at Maui Memorial Hospital. "I'll see you when I get home if you're still up."

"Mahalo, Mom," shouted her daughter Makalani from her upstairs bedroom.

"Thank you, Auntie," echoed Kekoa, from the family room, where he was watching TV.

Kekoa finished watching the *American Masters* show on PBS about Duke Kahanamoku and learned a lot about the famous surfer and Olympic swimmer that he didn't know before—such as him being an ali'i, a Hawaiian of noble birth, going back before the overthrow—*coup d'état*, actually—of Queen Lili'uokalani, the Kingdom's last reigning monarch. If the program had ever been shown in America, he had never seen it.

He switched over to the local news, which was just starting. Usual island stuff.

Owners with rooms or houses formerly listed with AirBnB were still whining that a recent change in the law put an end to short-term transient housing in residential neighborhoods. More than 1,300 properties had been de-listed from the organization.

Olowalu Beach was closed due to a shark sighting.

Average number of tourists on Maui was currently 61,272.

Some tourist fell from a Ka'anapali Beach high-rise. Was it an accident or foul play? *I feel sorry for anyone down below who heard the splat. Tsk. I've got to stop that. Yeah, I know, it's just gallows humor, but somebody loved him.*

Weekly weather report was the usual Maui forecast. Eighty-five to 88 each day for a week, seven 72s at night, rain likely in Hāna.

"Kekoa," his cousin called, "let's eat. I'm going out tonight and want to eat before I get ready."

"Want to make sure there's no chewed spinach stuck in your teeth, right?"

"Yep, that's it," was the sarcastic reply.

"You don't want to wait for your brother?"

"'A'ole. He's working some road-construction job, installing guardrails somewhere on Hāna Highway. There's no telling when he'll be home."

Kekoa set the table, put large Corelle soup bowls on matching plates, and dished up two servings of what he guessed was a stew: sliced Portuguese sausage, potatoes, onion, and cabbage that had all been simmered in chicken broth for three hours. *Damn, it smells good.*

Makalani came into the kitchen and scanned the table. "Do you want bread?"

"No, thank you."

"Well, I do," she said and took the loaf and the butter from the refirgerator.

"Going drinking tonight?"

"Why would you ask *that*?" Maka replied, but her tone gave her away.

"It was a simple 'yes' or 'no' question, so when you answer a question with another question, I get suspicious." When he saw she wasn't going to look up to meet his eyes, he continued, "I am a trained investigator, you know. So, when I see my beautiful seventeen-year-old cousin—who I know avoids carbs like the plague—loading up on bread, which she hopes will soak up the alcohol, and lathering it with butter, which she thinks will coat her stomach lining and also delay absorption, I come to one conclusion. That she plans to consume adult beverages tonight. Am I right?" *I won't tell her she's right on both counts.*

She looked up as the next piece of sausage went to her mouth, but the sheepish expression was an admission.

"In case you forgot, I was seventeen once myself."

"Don't tell Mom, please. I'm letting you use my car."

"Oh, extortion now?" he asked, smiling. "No, if you get home by midnight and aren't drunk, I won't say anything. But, Maka, while your dad's out on the ship, I will have a few words with Nalu when he gets here."

"Really?" she asked, incredulous.

"Count on it. And thanks for letting me use your car."

He couldn't hear what she said but was pretty certain she was cussing under her breath as she stormed out of the room.

"Don't worry—I'll do the dishes," he hollered from the bottom of the stairs, laughing.

Kekoa was rinsing the bowls, wondering if Lia would wear the string bikini again, when he saw his cousin Nalu coming home from work.

✦ ✦ ✦

CHAPTER 4

TWO WEEKS EARLIER

WHEN DEL KURTZ awoke the next morning, it was still dark, but he didn't want to be seen getting out of the truck by mall employees arriving for work. He got dressed and pulled a clean but wrinkled shirt from his backpack. Rather than go through that pretzel maneuver at the tailgate, he slid into the cab. Nothing of value in the glove box, but, hanging from an adapter in the cigarette lighter was a cell-phone charging cord. *This just keeps getting better and better!* He would have to hotwire the truck tonight, if it had any battery left, to start the engine and charge his phone. He had been using outside electrical outlets at businesses but always feared getting rousted by some cop or security guard.

He scanned the area to the left and front. He saw the shopping cart full of crap alongside the stairwell in the opposite corner but no people. Not knowing if it would stick or squeak, he softly opened the door and stepped out. No sooner had he gently pushed the door shut than he jumped from fright and was embarrassed that he'd emitted a rather loud gasp. The bag lady was standing next to the truck, just behind the driver's door. *How long has she been there? How did I not see her?* Before his adrenaline had subsided, she said something.

"Where did you come from?" he demanded, although the answer was obvious. Then he remembered having heard her say something. "What did you say?"

"I want five dollars rent."

He was about to curse her but decided to be neighborly. "This isn't your truck, or you'd be sleeping in it. So how d'ya figure I owe you rent?"

"Rent for me not sayin' anything t'da security guard you broke inta dat truck," she said through her remaining teeth.

Del saw a car pulling into the parking garage down at the other end, so, before she could make a scene, he turned away to pull out his cash, peel off a five, and jam it into her dirty paw.

She examined the bill and shuffled back toward her cart. Del scowled at her back, shouldered his backpack, and went to look for a cheap restaurant.

✦ ✦ ✦

CHAPTER 5

IT WAS BARELY daybreak when Lia pulled onto the shoulder behind the old Ford Bronco with a rack over the roof. She had intended to beat him there, if he actually showed up, but guessed he'd had the same idea. *Oh, well.*

The pre-dawn coolness had prompted her to wear a zippered sweatshirt, and she felt the chill even more here, maybe because the cool air over the warm water was creating its own light fog.

She saw him before she came out of the woods, looking out past the cliff, to where the waves were breaking. He turned around quickly as soon as he heard her and then seemed to relax.

"Aloha kakahiaka, e Malia."

She had thought she would try calling him "Kekoa" today, but not now that he hadn't used her nickame.

"Good morning, Justin. Is that all you're wearing? No rash guard or anything?"

"You didn't have one the other day. Besides, the weather report said the water is 78 degrees. That's like bath water. In California, there's like two weeks in August when you don't need a wetsuit if you're going to stay out more than fifteen minutes."

"Hiki nō," she said as she unzipped and removed the sweatshirt and let the cutoffs slide down her tan legs.

Somewhat disappointed, he saw she was wearing a black Spandex one-piece, not the skimpy blue number from before. It was cut high on the sides, accentuating her long limbs, and had an open back crossed by black straps in a double"X." The whole look served only to confirm the girl definitely had a killer figure.

"Mākaukau?" she asked, picking up her board and walking to the water.

Yes, I'm ready, he thought, wondering if she threw out Hawaiian words just to test him, because he didn't sense she did it to show off. But he did enjoy the view as he followed her into the shorebreak. Across the Alalākeiki Channel, the sun coming over Haleakalā was lighting the morning on Kahoʻolawe.

They stayed out for nearly ninety minutes, almost always able to catch the same wave, one following the other. Kekoa saw that Lia was an accomplished surfer but glad she said she had to go in because he was worn out but didn't want to be the first to call it quits.

For her part, Lia enjoyed having someone to surf with for a change. Kekoa was a good surfer. He probably learned early and maintained his skill in California, but he didn't try showing off or other macho craziness to impress her.

They stood up when they reached the shallow water, carried the boards to the beach, and peeled off the Velcro straps of their leashes.

"Looks like we have some company," Lia said, pointing her chin up the beach to the left.

"Sure do," Kekoa agreed, looking at the green sea turtle. "Are you in a hurry? Want to go for breakfast?" he asked.

"No, thank you. I have things to do, but I generally lie here for awhile to dry off."

"Okay. I'll join you."

They turned the front of the boards makai, so, even though the fins sank into the sand a little, the back was still somewhat elevated. They could lie on the boards and still see the water.

"So, you here on vacation? Or just came to visit your tūtū? Or what?"

"Four weeks' vacation . . . *and* visiting family. The county said I had too much vacation time saved up, so I needed to burn some off or they'd quit giving me more."

"You keep a board here?"

"Nahh, borrowed it from my cousin, Nalu. Same with the car, but a different cousin—his sister." He waited to see if she would comment, before continuing, "Most of my family still . . ."

With her eyes still closed, she reached out and laid a hand softly on his arm. It was the second time she had touched him, and he experienced the same jolt as he had the previous day.

"Shhh. Just lie here and absorb the sun," she whispered and withdrew her hand.

After several minutes of relative quiet—well, except for water lapping the shore, birds in the woods, palms fronds scratching together, and the occasional car going by out on the road, Kekoa heard Lia stir. She was getting up.

"Time for me to go." She had already picked up her sweatshirt and was bending over to pick up the board, giving him a great cleavage shot, whether intentional or not.

"To do what?" he asked, not being nosy but just to delay her a moment longer or finagle an invitation to come along.

"Are you being a cop again? I said I had things to do."

He nearly asked, "What things?" but decided *that* would have sounded like an interrogation, settling for, "Thanks for inviting me to surf this morning. See you again some time."

She stopped. "I'm sorry—that was curt. Hardly kapu aloha, huh?

"On mornings I don't work at the store, I teach remedial mathematics—arithmetic—to grade-school kids who are falling behind. Afternoons, I teach a math-prep class for high-school kids getting ready to take their SAT or ACT exam.

"As for the invitation, he mea ike." With that, she left.

KEKOA SPENT THE cool part of the morning weeding his aunt's garden. He saw some tomatoes were ready for harvesting. He brought them in, rinsed them off, and left them in a soup bowl on the counter. He waited until late in the morning to return to the coffee shop and was pleased to see Lia was working. He had to wait behind a gaggle of tourists who couldn't make up their minds what they wanted before he got to the counter.

"You again?" she teased even though they had already made eye contact.

"Let me take you to lunch."

"Why would I do that?"

He shrugged his shoulder and lifted his eyebrows, as if wondering himself.

"Because you like the fact I'm attracted to you, and you enjoy teasing me." *In more ways than one.*

Lia grinned but didn't contradict him as she looked over his shoulder at new customers examining the menu board. He turned, saw them, and ordered an iced coffee.

"Last time you ordered hot coffee."

"Do you remember the orders of all your customers?"

"No, just the ones I pay for," she smirked.

He laughed. "All the more reason to let me repay the favor and take you to lunch."

"OK. I only get thirty minutes, so it has to be somewhere close."

"I heard there's this new fish truck in those corner shops across from the fire station. I was told the owners bring in fresh catch every day. Wanna try their fish tacos?"

A stalker alarm triggered in her brain. The fire station was at the corner of her block! *Did he follow me home or do some cop stuff to find out where I live?*

"I'm kinda partial to the tacos at Pā'ia Fish Market, so maybe I'll do a comparison," she said, in the back of her mind wondering if she'd accepted his invitation too quickly.

"It's too far to walk, given the short time. My car is across the street in the Times lot."

Given their short window, Kekoa didn't want to waste time and did want to know more about this girl.

"So you grew up in Wailuku. What brought you to Kīhei?"

"Wailuku Heights, actually."

"Wow. Mauka of the highway?"

"'Ae, but that's why I usually just say 'Wailuku,' 'cause as soon as you add the 'Heights,' people get the wrong impression and think you're loaded. My parents bought it in the '60s, when my dad was still in the service, and they were the second owners even then."

"But the view must be great."

"It is, and we're not even near the top of the hill."

"So why Kīhei?"

"To be closer to the water. There's nothing to rent in Makena, which is where I like to surf, but there're tons of beaches in Kīhei so I can stand-up board to some of them, drive if I have to, and still be close to my jobs."

"Ha! You do stand-up, too."

"If it's in or on the water, I do it. Do you dive or snorkel?"

"Love snorkeling."

"Let's go sometime."

She sounded sincere; he'd make a point of going with her soon.

✦ ✦ ✦

CHAPTER 6

THIS CAMPING OUT thing was working well exccpt for that smelly, old bitch every morning. Did she ever sleep? She certainly hadn't bathed in years. Del Kurtz had discovered that no security guards patrolled the parking garage on foot, at least after the mall closed, but a security-patrol vehicle drove through around 10 p.m., after the last of the shopkeepers had departed, and again around midnight, when the last movies got out. If they made any other drive-bys, he was sleeping.

Between the 10:00 and midnight patrols, he hot-wired the pickup and ran it long enough to recharge his phone and, probably, the truck's own battery. *The damn owner should thank me he won't come back to a dead battery. I just hope he doesn't return when I'm inside!*

His phone alarm woke him at 5:45, and he was out of the truck by six. After the first time, he knew to look for the bag lady, who was always waiting for her extortion money. Today was different, though. When he went to hand her the five, she said she now wanted ten dollars. He told her to go fuck herself and didn't even give her the five; he walked off for his morning jaunt to Burger King to start the day. The rest of the day was spoiled by him worrying about the old hag spoiling his swell camper digs.

That night, he went to the new Tom Cruise movie at the mall theater. His showing got out at 11:00, but another didn't finish until after midnight. Many people parked in the lot, so the garage was almost deserted, but, when he walked into the garage, the old lady crawled out from her cave under the stairs.

"I missed da last guard, but I'm telling the next one about you," she hollered from acoss the garage.

He motioned with his hands for her to lower her voice as she walked across the garage toward her shopping cart she used to partially conceal her hideout. He even pulled some money out of his pocket and waved it in the air to shut her up.

"I don't want your stinkin' money anymore. I'm tired of ya bein' here and wakin' me up every night runnin' da truck."

She must have read the look on is face, because she started backing up; when he was almost to her cart, she turned, crawled under the stairs, and started shrieking.

"Shut up, you old hag!" He crawled under the steps after her and got an arm around her neck. She kept yelling, but the volume was reduced by her windpipe being constricted. He lifted her up high enough to bash her head against the bottom of a stair, a metal form filled with concrete. She emitted an "ugh," and he was able to roll her over and sit on her several layers of clothes over a large stomach. He got his hands around her throat but was impeded by some other cloth. When he became aware she had a scarf around her neck, he tightened that with all his strength. He felt her legs kicking and bucking under him, but he didn't care anymore. He hoped no one heard her, but he was aroused now and couldn't stop—she had to be punished for causing him trouble.

He unbuttoned his pants and pulled down his zipper to release his throbbing cock. Rushing, he haphazardly pushed up several dresses and pulled down her filthy, old-lady underwear. It took a bit of work to penetrate her, but once he did he jammed himself into her again and again until he was satisfied. As with the hooker, he didn't like those dead eyes looking at him, accusing him; he covered them with her hands.

After he got himself put back together, he dragged her onto what looked like her bed, a pile of cardboard and rags, straightened her dresses, threw the underwear into the dark under the lowest step, and covered her with the ragged blankets. She probably had some cash stashed in her pockets or elsewhere, but he was damned if he could put up with her stink for another second. He looked in every direction before he crawled out, pushed the junk-filled Target shopping cart to cover the largest part of the "campsite" entrance, and casually walked back to the truck.

Tomorrow he would take the truck and leave the area.

JOSEPH ULUFANUA DROVE his miniature street sweeper down the ramp from the middle deck of the parking garage to finish cleaning on the bottom floor, a process he followed three times a week. He started on the top at the crack of dawn so there was enough natural light when he finished on the bottom. Cars had been left here overnight again—two on the top deck, one in the middle. He always wondered why. *Did it not start? Did the driver go home with a lover?*

He saw the Datsun pickup was gone. He knew it had parked here with permission. *I guess that guy from Lids came home from his trip to Japan.* He swung his machine into that corner and saw that the bag lady was still camping under the stairs in the other corner. It wasn't his garage, so it didn't bother him, and she had her shopping cart tucked up nice and tight out of his way. He just wished she would find a place to bathe because the smell coming out of there was really rank this morning.

He spun his machine around her cart as fast as he could and moved quickly away, holding his breath the entire time.

✦ ✦ ✦

CHAPTER 7

"**Y**OU AGAIN? LUCKY for me my boss called in sick. I'm the on-duty manager again."

"So the other two girls can handle the store while you go to lunch?"

"They could. Are you asking me out?"

"Yes. How can I do the taco test if I don't go to Pā'ia while the memory of the food truck is still on my taste buds?"

Lia laughed. "You're funny. OK, but it has to be quick again." She spoke to her two helpers and came around the counter. "You parked at Times again?"

"Yep."

Traffic was busy, and, when a small break appeared, he took her hand and led her quickly across the street. The slight demonstration of dominance surprised her, but she liked it.

When they got close to the restaurant, she directed him to the best place to park in the back. Thankfully, the line was super short. They ordered, he paid, she took the plastic number for their table, and he carried their drinks.

Even though she seemed to know a lot of Hawaiian—maybe she was even fluent (he'd have to find out)—Kekoa could tell by her command of English that she was very well read or was college educated or both, so he asked her, "Where did you go to college?"

"Who said I did?"

"No one, but I can tell by your vocabulary and the way you speak and carry yourself—it often implies higher education."

"They teach you that in cop school?"

He laughed. "It's called a police academy. No, mostly from life experience."

She smiled to herself. *Why do I enjoy teasing this guy so much?*

"I went to UH-Maui for three years. Accounting major."

"Oh, yeah? Like what kind of courses do you need for that?"

"Quantitative reasoning, business computing, business analytics, microeconomics, statistics, financial accounting, managerial accounting, income measurements and asset valuation—"

Kekoa held up both palms toward her. "OK, I get it. A lot of boring classes."

She feigned shock. "I'm hurt. That's my future you're making fun of!"

"Oh, Lia, I'm sorry. I wasn't making fun of it."

She laughed. "You're so easy; I was kidding. Yeah, it sounds boring to you, but numbers are like solving puzzles for me. Like solving crimes is for you, I guess. Did you see that movie *The Accountant*?"

He searched his memory for a second. "The one with Anna Kendrick and what's his name . . . Ben Affleck?"

"You remember the female lead but not the star?"

"Well, she's cute."

Lia gave a little snort. "Anyway, remember when he comes to that office and works all night going through all those files, looking for numbers that don't add up or aren't where they're supposed to be?"

"Yeah."

"That's what accountants do! Doesn't that sound exciting?"

He chuckled, looking to make sure she wasn't teasing him again. "No, not really."

This time she laughed out loud. "That's OK. I do, without being high-functioning autistic."

"You mean you're not?" he asked seriously until he cracked a grin.

She slapped the hand he had resting on the table. "Brat."

The food had already been delivered two minutes ago. "Eat your taco before it gets any colder," she said, and they both went to work on them.

+ + +

CHAPTER 8

Debbie Caldwell thought today had been the best day of her scheduled weeklong trip. Hawai'i, or Maui, to be precise, was everything she'd hoped for and more than she expected. Despite what she had read on some of the anti-tourist blogs and Facebook sites, most of the locals had been very nice to her, and the others had been at least civil. She did not want to be the "ugly American" in their homeland, nor did she act like Maui was her personal Disneyland.

She had purchased and studied a small Hawaiian-English dictionary before she left home and carried it in her backpack. She felt pretty confident in her pronunciation of the vowels and diphthongs. She enjoyed saying "aloha" and "mahalo" even if it wasn't reciprocated.

She skipped Hertz and the other big agencies and rented a good used car from a local Turo operator. She tried to buy local whenever possible, avoiding corporate chain stores and restaurants. She loved poi and was developing a taste for tuna poke, although raw fish had never been her thing, even back home in Elizabethtown, New Jersey.

Debbie didn't want to waste one minute and was squeezing as much activity into her days as she could. Who knew when she could afford to return? Third-grade schoolteachers didn't make a lot of money, but she did appreciate the umbrella of health insurance. So far, she had walked all over Lāhainā, the capital of the Hawaiian Kingdom until 1845, she had learned, toured the whaling museum, and seen the largest banyan tree in the United States. Well, if you considered Hawaiʻi a state, which, she had learned, many Hawaiians do not as a result of their queen being overthrown by the U.S. in the late 1800s.

After walking in and out of all the little "tourist traps," art galleries, and specialty boutiques on Front Street, she had eaten supper at a popular fish restaurant and then gone to see a recommended magic show. Friends had told her not to miss it, and she wasn't disappointed. It was as much a comedy show, but the sleight-of-hand tricks in the small theater were amazing, and the jokes had her laughing until her sides hurt. *No wonder it sells out every night*, she thought.

It was already dark by the time she found the place she planned to camp on the beach south of the town. She knew overnight camping on the beach was a no-no, but she decided to risk it to keep within her budget. She had scouted out a place earlier in the day on the way north near where some other small tents were located. The spot she picked was well above the high-water mark but not next to the highway. She didn't want some drunk driving off the road and crushing her little one-man pop-up—with her in it—or being flooded by some rogue wave.

The next morning, she was up well before dawn. She got dressed over her two-piece and drove to the Kīhei Canoe Club, located on the north end of the town. Travelocity gave its visitor-paddle rave reviews, and one of them mentioned they had showers. It was cold, convenient, and free, which was all fine with her. She was parked right at the club and was dried and dressed and still fluffing out her damp hair before any of the members or visitors started arriving.

She had made her reservation online, so the check-in process was easy. The woman told her what canoe she would be in, said "Nick" would be her hoʻokele, or captain, and pointed her to a door, where she was measured for her paddle and was reminded by the friendly man to return it to the same place.

Thirty or forty minutes later, the yellow and red canoes were pushed on rollers off the top of the beach almost to the water's edge. Nick and a woman called "the stroker" explained the proper way to get in and get out of the canoe safely, showed them how to hold the paddle, how to "stab" it in the water and pull it back, when to switch to the other side of the canoe to paddle, and other safety reminders. There were life vests on-board, but no one was required to wear one unless they chose to. Hers was a "double canoe," two hulls lashed together with wooden braces, called ʻiako, but far enough apart that crew members in both hulls could paddle on either side.

Finally, the captain, who had assigned paddlers according to weight and experience, while still trying to keep couples and families near each other, told everyone to stand by their seat and grab the back of their seat with one hand. Everyone was anxious to go, but the captain kept waiting, watching the waves coming in, and, suddenly, he yelled, "OK, now!"

Slow at first and then faster, the canoe slid into the water, and one-by-one, front-to-back as they had been instructed, the paddlers got into the canoe and started paddling. It took a minute or two, with the captain calling out corrections to people by their seat numbers, before everyone got in time. The two strokers in the front of both canoes set the pace of how fast they paddled, and the one on her side made the call with a "hut," followed by a stroke, than a "ho," followed by another stroke before everyone switched their paddle to the other side of their hull.

Debbie thought it was one of the most fun and yet invigorating activities she had ever done. It really felt like Hawai'i. They paddled south and stopped at a turtle "cleaning station," a place where the green sea turtles congregated at a reef to have their shells cleaned by certain fish. They saw several "honu" when the big reptiles came up for breath, and one swam right under the canoe. On the way there, the captain had stopped and led a chant welcoming the sun that had already risen over Mauna Haleakalā, the huge dormant volcano.

After resuming paddling, the captain steered the canoe to a beach, where they landed and could get out; they walked over to see an ancient fishpond enclosed with a wall of stacked rocks. A number of turtles were there, as well. It was low tide, and the captain told them they could wade out for a closer look at several turtles sunning themselves on the inside wall of the fishpond but to stay at least ten feet away.

While chatting with paddlers from the other canoes that had also landed at the beach, she shared about her trip so far and mentioned needing to find a place to camp that night. One of the club members told her to keep it to herself but she could probably camp for one night at the club's other site, less than a mile north of where the canoes were parked. The canoes reloaded, pushed off, and paddled back to the club, where the hardest part of the morning was rolling the canoes back up the short grade to their resting places.

After rinsing and returning her paddle and saying goodbye, Debbie drove up to the other place, saw there was room to park alongside the road, a nice place to pitch her tent, and then took off in her rental car to do some sightseeing before returning just before sunset.

The next morning, she was up before dawn, packed her gear, quickly broke down her small tent, and quietly left the canoe yard. She filled up at Costco on her way out of Kahului, ate breakfast at a nearby food truck, and was occasionally able to see the sun rising out of the ocean as she drove around the curves and in and out of the rainforest on the famous Hāna Highway. She crossed the many one-lane bridges, saw numerous waterfalls, and finally reached the turn to Wai'ānapanapa State Park, where she had made her reservation two months ago.

Her first chore was setting up and staking down her little tent. Easier to do in the daylight. Then she put on her suit and went swimming in the lovely, black sand cove. After drying off, she changed into shorts and a T-shirt, checked her backpack for water, sunscreen, mosquito repellant, and snacks, zipped up her tent door, and continued around the island to the Haleakalā National Park. She showed her NP membership card at the guard booth, proceeded to the parking lot, and set out on the two-mile uphill hike to the Pīpīwai Trail bamboo forest. The fifteen- to twenty-foot canes blocked much of the sun, and an occasional breeze caused the tips to rattle together in some kind of eerie wind chime. As she traversed the narrow, raised walkway, the tall, dense bamboo stalks on both sides of the path seem to close in on her. *This place is kind of spooky*, she thought.

She had to step across slippery stones to cross a creek twice before reaching the trail's end at Waimoku Falls, where three silvery ribbons fell down the face of the 400-foot lava cliff.

After the hike back down to her car, Debbie used the restrooom and read the historical and educational displays at the ranger station, before retracing the winding ten-mile route back to Hāna, stopped at the Hasagawa General Store to restock on snacks, and then treated herself to a dinner at a sit-down restaurant.

Back at camp, she took a shower and washed her summer-short hair. Normally shoulder length, she'd had her stylist cut off a few inches before this trip. She sat at a picnic table and kept fluffing her hair so it would dry faster. Some of the other campers came by to chat, every-one exchanging stories of where they were from and what sights they had seen on vacation. The sun wasn't visible from here, but she watched the sky grow darker, and, about the time the first stars popped out, she crawled into her tent and zipped the door closed.

✦ ✦ ✦

CHAPTER 9

THE PICKUP'S GAS gauge read "full" when Del Kurtz pulled out of the parking garage in the early-morning darkness. He pulled over to a curb outside the mall area and used a bottle of water and some old newspapers to wash all the dust off the windshield.

Burger King wasn't open, but he decided to stick to his routine and parked in the lot until they opened at six. While he waited, he opened his backpack and removed the brochures he had picked up before leaving the airport.

The *Maui Driving Map* would be handy, and he flipped it up on the dash. One of the items wasn't a brochure but more of a thin magazine, *101 Things to Do in Maui*. The ʻĪao Needle looked like something worth seeing. He found it on the map and saw it wasn't far from where he was. No, he didn't want to go to a rodeo in Makawao or a stock-car race in Puʻunene.

Hmm, he had heard about the Road to Hāna. Yeah, that would be someplace to go; take a nice leisurely drive and find out what the hype was all about.

He took the magazine into Burger King to look at the other choices among the 101 while he ate his breakfast and drank his coffee. What the hell was a silversword plant, and who came to Maui just to see one? Not him, anyway. Before he left, he got his free refill, asked for a plastic lid, and took a handful of napkins from the dispenser on the way out.

The road he needed to start on was right in front of the restaurant, so he turned right out of the lot and made his way into the rising sun. At a stoplight, he dug around in the glove box and found an old pair of sunglasses. He guessed the owner must have taken his good ones with him. These glasses were scratched, but they would save him from going blind. Traffic was heavy, mostly with cars and trucks—*there sure are a lot of pickups here*—heading into the city for work.

His first stop was the town of Pā'ia. He had to find a place to pee. It looked like a bunch of small stores and restaurants aimed at tourists like he saw in Lāhainā. He bought bottled water and enough snacks to qualify to obtain the code for a cipher lock on a bathroom shared by several businesses.

He next pulled in at Twin Falls because he saw all the tourists stopping. He knew he looked out of place with his jeans and high-top shoes when everyone else had shorts and flipflops. So what if his legs were bone white? It looked like that was true of a lot of the tourists. It required a hike up a well-worn path, but he saw the falls, two of them, of course, but not that big. A number of tourists were already in the water swimming under the falls.

Back on the road, he just took his time and followed the tourist convoy. *So, this is a rainforest.* It looked like a plain old woods to him. When he saw a bunch of cars pulled over at the narrow bridges to see waterfalls, he did, too, if there was any room to park. Some of the falls were taller, and the water was gushing over the top of the fall. *That's where all the rain goes,* he realized.

There was a rest stop on the left, so he pulled in to use the bathroom again. Across the highway were stairs that went to some kind of viewing area, so he went for a look. As he expected, more waterfalls.

Much farther, he saw a sign for a lava-tube tour. He always liked caves and turned off the highway down a potholed road. The attraction came up pretty fast, and he pulled in. The entrance fee wasn't much. He discovered it was a self-guided tour; signs inside would explain things. So, after the vendor gave him and the others who had stopped some brief instructions and had them sign a release, they were handed flashlights and sent on their way. It was obviously a low-budget operation, but he found the signs informative. He didn't have to wait for the slowest reader in the group and thought it was worth the price of admission.

When he entered Hāna, he passed the fire station, drove through town—there wasn't much to it that he saw—turned around, and came back. He stopped and filled up on tacos from a food truck just off the road. The tacos were pretty good but nothing like the Mexicans make in California. Continuing back through town, he saw a gas station and checked his fuel gauge. Still above three-quarters of a tank. *This little truck sure gets good mileage.*

A general store with a Japanese name was on his right. It had been in the *101 Things* magazine he had looked at, so he pulled in. *So this is what a general store is.* It was like a grocery store, hardware store, sporting-goods store, and tourist trap all jammed into one building. He bought an ice-cream sandwich and a bag of M&Ms for later.

He followed the road down to the water, but it looked more like a harbor than a beach. His magazine said something about a red-sand beach, but he didn't know where it was, except not here. The gravel parking lot was pretty big, so he found a place in the shade, put the windows down, and sat there watching young kids surf.

Del didn't know how long he had slept, but when he awakened, the surfers were gone, and the shade had moved all the way to the water. Knowing how long it took to drive that narrow, winding road, he estimated there was no way to make it back to the city before dark and decided to look for a place to park for the night.

He took out his map and saw there was a state park not far from Hāna. Wai'ānapanapa. *I wonder how you pronounce that. Maybe, wah-ee-ana-pan-apa.* "Oh, hell—who cares?" he told himself and started the truck.

The place wasn't hard to find. When he went down the road, he saw the guard shack and stopped to pay the entrance fee. He saw signs that said reservations and permits were required to camp overnight. Well, he wasn't really camping, just sleeping in his truck. What were they going to do, make him leave? He'd just find another place to park.

He pulled into the parking lot and could see, farther west, where all the tents were set up, and it looked like there were some cabins, too. He got out and followed the trail down to the beach, a black-sand beach. He'd never seen one of those before. Dusk was approaching, and he could smell campers cooking their dinner. He continued on and followed the signs to the blowhole. He stood there and waited for waves to come in and watched the water shoot out like a miniature geyser three or four times.

Del was getting self-conscious about always wearing jeans and urban hikers when everyone else was in shorts and bathing suits and flipflops. *Who cares if I have white legs—so do a lot of these other tourists. What do I care what they think? I'm never going to see them again. I have my suit, but I need something for my feet.*

When he found the Honor Fruit Stand near the parking lot, he picked out a couple of fruits he recognized and paid more than the suggested price. He was an honorable person, after all.

A young boy, maybe eight or nine, was looking over the colorful offerings, and Del asked, "Hey, kid—where's a good place to buy flipflops?"

The boy followed Del's line of sight down to his feet. "Oh, you mean slippers! They're everywhere. If you're going to Hāna, they have them at the general store, but Walmart, Long's, anywhere."

"OK, thanks."

The kid nodded and headed back toward the tents.

Del leaned against the metal railing, eating his apple and watching a young woman with bright reddish-orange hair and a green swimming suit coming back from the beach and wrapping a large beach towel around herself. Her little tent was down below the overlook where he was standing. She bent over to unzip the door of the tent, demurely holding the front of the towel closed above her breasts. She came out moments later with what looked like folded clothes and, still wrapped in the towel, walked toward the public showers. He envisioned what she looked like in the shower and whether she was a natural redhead.

✦ ✦ ✦

CHAPTER 10

KEKOA SAW HER as soon as he came in and smiled. She was at the Order station, and there were a number of customers ahead of him. He saw her smile as soon as she saw him in the line.

"What can I get you, sir?" she smirked.

He smirked back. "Small black coffee."

He paid in cash. When she came with his change, she held the back of his hand in one of hers and put the change in his palm with the other, looking at him the entire time.

"Go to dinner with me tonight."

"OK. Let me call you as soon as I get off. Give me your number."

Well, that was easy, he thought. He removed a business card from his wallet and wrote his personal number on the back with her pen.

She looked at the star badge on the front of the card. "So official," she teased.

He grinned, nodded, and moved down to the Pick Up Here station.

When the young girl—she looked like a high schooler—gave him his coffee, he asked, "What time does Lia's shift end?"

"We both get off at four."

"Thanks."

HIS PHONE RANG at 4:34.

"Hi."

"Did you assume it was going to be me?"

"Of course. Who else would be calling?"

"Your mom or dad calling to say hi. Your grandmother calling to invite you to dinner.

"Your cousin wanting her car back. Your girlfriend calling to check on you."

"My parents don't call me, I call them. Tūtū called me, actually returned my call, and invited me to dinner the second night I was here. The day I saw you at the beach. There is no girlfriend at home." He knew the last item was the one she was interested in.

"So, here I am, calling, like you asked. Did you want to do something?"

"Yes, I want to take you to dinner."

"OK. Did you have someplace in mind? I think it's too late to get reservations at Mama's Fish House." He knew she was kidding. Mama's was well-known for its oceanfront dining and being one of the most expensive restaurants on Maui. Tables needed to be booked months in advance.

He might have joined in her laugh but didn't want her to think that he thought she wasn't worth it.

"I was thinking of Kō at the Fairmont. Sound good?"

"Sounds fine," she said, genuinely impressed. "Can we still get in?"

"Yes. I already made a reservation in case you approved."

"Good planning."

"Thanks. Can you be ready by 6:15? They close at eight, and if we get down there right away, we might be in time for the sunset."

"'Ae, hiki au. See you then—oh, and you have to park on the street. I use the only parking space."

✦ ✦ ✦

CHAPTER 11

KEKOA PULLED ONTO the dirt shoulder alongside a stone wall at the address she had given him. She lived down the street from the fire station, just past the library. He had barely turned off the engine and was about to get out of the Bronco when she came around the wall from her driveway. Expecting the usual "I'll be ready in five minutes," a woman on time was a surprise but not near as big a surprise as she was.

She looked like a model. Her sun-bleached "dirty blond" hair was pulled back in a pony tail, accenting her long neck. A white lisianthus blossom was worn above her right ear. She was wearing a tropical cocktail dress with a black background covered with large, overlapping 'ulu leaves in three shades of green. A deep "V" cut in the front tastefully displayed her assets without being overly revealing. The dress stopped well above her knees, displaying her long, bare legs all the way to the black pumps.

She was halfway to the SUV before he reached her, and they exchanged traditional honis. It was the first time he had seen her wearing any makeup, minimal as it was: eyeliner, eye shadow, mascara, pale lipstick. *Not that she needed it*, he thought. She was also wearing some provocative perfume.

"Lia, you're stunning."

"Mahalo nui," she said, somewhat bashfully. "You clean up pretty well yourself."

He was only wearing some of the limited wardrobe he had brought with him: a beige, tropical-weight sport coat over a dark polo shirt, clean khakis, black socks, and loafers.

"Thank you for this," she said. They were still standing face to face, the late-afternoon sun behind her.

"For what?"

"Asking me out—taking me someplace I can get dressed up for a change. I forget I like this part of being a woman, too, sometimes."

"Well, it's my pleasure."

He put his hand on the small of her back and turned her toward the Bronco. It was then he saw the back of the dress was styled even deeper, her tan skin bare from her neck to the bottom of the "V." It actually took his breath away.

He didn't question their luck for a reservation made the same day, but they did get a table at the window and actually were seated before the sunset but were disappointed to discover the ocean couldn't be seen from the restaurant and enjoyed a good laugh over glasses of wine from the bottle they had mutually decided upon. She was watching the sun to see where it would set; he was mostly watching her.

"We wouldn't have seen Green Flash anyway; the sun's going to set behind Mauna Kahālāwai." He nodded.

"How tall are you?" she asked out of the blue.

"Six-one."

"Hmm, three inches taller than me."

"So, if I'm 25, how many years am I more or less than you?"

"Is that your surreptitious way to ask a woman her age, or are you just testing my math skills? You know I'm an accounting major . . . if I ever finish school."

"How many years do you have left?"

"Just one," she replied. "One-half the number of years I'm younger than you." In case he was curious, she added, "I ran out of money and didn't want to take out any student loans, so I skipped last semester. My savings are almost enough for tuition and graduation fees."

"Good luck. I hope you make it."

"What about you?" she asked. "Where did you live growing up, and where did you go to school?"

"We lived in Wailuku and went to school at St. Anthony's. I spent most summers down here at my grandmother's. My dad was in the Navy, a pharmacist's mate, and was due to get out. They said they'd pay his way to college if he re-enlisted, so he said he'd do it if they stationed him at Pearl Harbor so he could go to pharmacy school at UH. He graduated when I was a junior, got promoted, and was transferred to the Balboa Naval Hospital in San Diego.

"My Dad married his high-school sweetheart, and he and Mom have been together thirty years.

"My sister is two years older than me and had already started school at Maui College when we moved. I was in junior year at St. Anthony's. Billy was a freshman. Anyway, Janet got a degree in pharmacy at UC San Diego and works for CVS now. When my dad retires, they want to move back and work for Long's here, which, you probably know, is owned by CVS."

"Your family kept their home here?"

"'Ae, been renting it out all this time. That reminds me—one of my chores while I'm here is to stop by and do an inspection."

"Is your mom a maoli?"

"Oh, 'ae! Andrea Keli'ipuleole Kupa'a."

"Anyone else?" she asked.

"My kid brother, William. Two years younger. Ha! Same age as you. He's a paramedic with an ambulance company in San Diego."

"Anyone else?"

"Lots of aunts, uncles, and cousins. You already know my tūtū.

"So, what about you?" he asked.

"Well, our family's claim to fame is my four-times great-grandfather, Chester Davies. He was a carpenter on a whaling ship. They stopped in Lāhainā to refit on the way to the Bering Sea, and he broke his leg, or his arm, the stories vary. Anyway, he lost his job on the ship and found work in town, gradually accumulating his own tools and starting a carpentry business. That was in the 1820s, when Lāhainā was still the capital. Two of my later great-grandfathers signed the Kū'ē Petition. So, you see, we've been Hawaiians for 200 years.

"My dad died of cancer when I was in high school. He was a Marine for 20 years, retired as a Master Sergeant. It was Agent Orange exposure in Vietnam that killed him."

"I'm sorry," he said.

She shrugged. "Thank God he had good life insurance. My mom was able to pay off the house. My brother—I'm the youngest, he's in the middle—is a firefighter, good guy. He married a schoolteacher, but she stays home now, and they live in the house with their three kids. Our mom moved into the 'ohana in the back. Our older brother is a crack addict, and no one has seen him for years."

Justin lifted his wine glass. "Here's to Carpenter's Mate Chester Davies, without whom we would never have met."

Lia clinked hers against his, smiling at him over the long-stem glasses.

It was almost closing time when they finished. Lia looked over and saw the bill while Kekoa was getting out his credit card. Well, it wasn't L&L, the Hawaiian fast-food place in town.

As they left the restaurant, Lia asked, "Would you like to walk for a little bit?"

"Sure."

She took his arm. "Come with me."

They left the main building and weaved their way through the resort grounds to the beach.

"Polo Beach," she announced.

"I know. Remember, I grew up here."

She gave him a playful elbow in the ribs. Before they walked down the steps to the beach, she took off her heels. Justin removed his socks and shoes, and then took off his sports coat and draped it over her shoulders.

"Thank you, but I didn't say I was cold."

"I couldn't help but notice your headlights were on."

That earned him a backhand to the chest. "You shouldn't be looking there," she chided.

"I tried to be a gentleman and not appreciate your cleavage all night, but I couldn't help but see you were chilly."

"I always thought that if God was going to make me five foot ten, He might have given me a little more on top to keep it all in proportion."

"Trust me, your proportions are just fine."

THEY STROLLED THE short distance to the north end of the beach, reversed and walked to the south end, sometimes chatting but mostly just enjoying being together. Then they returned to the stairs and made their way to the car.

There wasn't any need to rush, in fact, Justin was happy to have time slow down, so he took Wailea Alanui to South Kīhei Road and stayed on it all the way through town to her turn. There was hardly any traffic.

"It's just after nine o'clock," he said.

"Maui Midnight," she added. They both laughed at the old joke.

Lia got out before he came around to open her door and draped his jacket over the back of her seat.

"Thank you for letting me wear your coat. I was getting a little cold toward the end of our walk."

"He mea iki," he replied. *It's a little thing.*

He followed her up the three steps to the little porch by her cottage door, where she turned to face him. With her heels on, he could look straight into her blue eyes.

"Thank you, Kekoa. I had a great time tonight. More than you can imagine. It was a really lovely meal, and I know it was expensive . . ."

"Worth every penny. Besides, it's a great ego boost for a guy when he walks in knowing he's with the best-looking woman in the place."

She smiled but shook her head with a little snort. "Stop."

She reached up with both hands and untied the bow of the white scarf holding her ponytail. He didn't think it was intentional, but he did notice the action momentarily lifted both of her breasts. She shook her hair, letting it fall down her back. One sun-bleached strand blew across her face. With the back of his fingers, he pushed it behind her ear.

She watched him do it and felt the gentleness in his touch as he moved the hair off her forehead. *What are you waiting for? Kiss me, you fool.*

From the top of her ear, his fingers slid down the side of her head and behind her neck where they stop and pulled her mouth to his, melding his body to hers. Their lips barely met for two seconds before she opened her mouth and their tongues danced together.

When it became obvious to both of them that he was getting turned on, she said, "Do you want to come in?" He heard the invitation in her voice but shook his head. "I better head out. Can I call you tomorrow?"

"Of course. Thank you again for a beautiful evening."

"Sure." He stopped at the bottom of the steps, turned back, and said, "You were the beautiful part," before walking to his vehicle.

✦ ✦ ✦

CHAPTER 12

It took DEL KURTZ a long time to fall asleep, as excited as he was about visiting the redhead. It was a good thing he set the alarm on his phone, or he may have slept until dawn. It was 2:45 in the morning, and he had decided 3:00 would be a good time to visit there.

He quietly lifted the camper door but did want to risk lowering the tailgate and making any noise, so he just climbed over it. He was afraid to walk barefoot, so only wore socks. He crossed the short distance to the end of the parking lot, silently walked to the metal railing and looked down at the tent. Lucky for him, it was at the end closest to him so he wouldn't have to pass any other campers. He just hoped no one came out to use the toilet or just pee in the bushes. He slowly descended the incline and moved to the tent. The zipper on the door was smooth, and even then, he opened it only a few inches at a time. The light of the half moon had been adequate for his approach, but once he was inside the tent, he had to wait and let his eyes adjust to the dark while he closed the door. She was asleep on her side, and the sleeping bag was unzipped halfway down. He'd have to be fast, before she screamed and awakened anyone.

The girl was either a very sound sleeper or totally exhausted. She must have been dreaming, too, because he saw her eyes moving under her closed lids as he slowly opened the sleeping bag the rest of the way. She was wearing only a T-shirt and panties. He would have to be quick.

He swung a leg over her hip and pushed her back flat under him, simultaneously getting both hands around her throat. He thought how he choked out that prostitute to silence her screams. There would be no screams from this one. She struggled and bucked beneath him and tried to turn her head sideways to get some air in her windpipe. He leaned in over her, adding the weight of his upper body into the pressure of his arms. It was dark but not pitch black in the tent, and he thought he saw her face turning blue. Then he saw her eyes bulging and knew it was nearly over.

After the body relaxed, he waited a minute with his hands still around her neck to ensure she was dead. Good, she was gone. He got off her, pulled down her underwear, and set it aside. To save time, he hadn't put on his own underwear when he woke in the camper. He pushed down his jeans and spread her legs. He was already hard and forced his way into the still-warm body. Yeah, her pubes were red. When he finished, he wiped himself off with her underwear and tossed them to the bottom of the tent. Her purse was against the wall of the tent, and he removed all the cash from her wallet; he found some more bills stuffed into one of her shorts' pockets.

After pulling up his jeans, he put her hands over her face and pulled up the sleeping bag zipper all the way to her shoulders to keep her hands in place. Slowly, he unzipped the tent's door, took a quick peek outside, and then crawled out, zipped it shut, and went back to his camper.

He was too amped to sleep, but he couldn't risk starting the truck and wakening any campers. He would take off in the morning, when the camp was beginning to stir, and follow out the first vehicle to leave.

Even with the little camper windows open and the truck windows cracked for ventilation, it was hot inside. He had stripped before he lay down but couldn't fall asleep. The more he thought about the red-haired girl thrashing about under him and the power of his hands around her neck, the more it excited him. He reached down, felt his throbbing cock, and jacked off into one of his dirty t-shirts.

+ + +

CHAPTER 13

LIA MADE ONLY three runs in some weak waves that any grom could have handled. It was fun while it lasted, but this rare southerly swell she had enjoyed for five days was petered out.

She was lying on her board, enjoying the heat of the rising sun and, she admitted, a little disappointed that Kekoa hadn't come out. Obviously not because there was no surf, but rather just to see and joke with him.

She had her fingers interlaced with her thumbs on her forehead, looking at the ao 'īlio, running dog clouds, wondering what he was doing right now. OK, if she was honest with herself, she was falling for him. It seemed obvious that he was interested in her. She hadn't been with anyone, romantically or sexually, in a while, and either one would be nice about now, but did she really want to get involved with someone who was leaving in less than a month?

Maybe she needed to talk to someone who knew him better.

THAT NIGHT AFTER work, she went home and examined the mangoes she had picked earlier in the day. They were nice, big Haden mangoes, their deep-purple skin ripened to a bright reddish-yellow. She chose the two ripest ones, peeled them, sliced the juicy orange flesh from the narrow seeds, and put it in a mixing bowl. After mashing the fruit, she added flour, sugar, three eggs, softened butter, a teaspoon of vanilla, baking powder, a dash of salt, a pinch of cinnamon, and another of nutmeg, and stirred it all together. While waiting for the oven to come up to 350⁰, she deftly lined her two meatloaf pans with aluminum foil, sprayed the inside with coconut oil, poured in the batter, and sprinkled kō pa'a, real cane sugar, lightly over the top. A bit later, the oven beeped. She shoved the pans to the center of the top rack and set the timer. Fifty minutes later, she pulled out the pans, checked with a chopstick that they were done, and set them on trivets.

After watching part of one of her TV shows, she took a shower and was on her way to bed when her phone buzzed. They talked for an hour.

JOE ULUFANUA WAS daydreaming about the weekend as he drove the sweeper down the ramp to the bottom deck. He had three other parking lots to get to before their businesses opened, and then he was off for the weekend. He and the missus had decided to take the kids and spend the weekend camping at Ukumehame beach.

As he neared the red shopping cart parked by the stairwell where the old lady slept, he was almost knocked over by the stench. He had emptied mouse traps enough times to know the odor of death. He also saw the dust on the handle of her shopping cart. It hadn't been moved in days. He thought mall security had been ignoring her, fearing some mentally unbalanced confrontation or maybe even misguided charity for a homeless person, but he had to inform someone today.

IT WAS FASTER and only a little longer to go up Kanani to the highway and take it to the "T" at Wailea Alanui drive before heading south, past Wailea Shops, the big resort hotels, and all the multi-million dollar homes, heading toward Makena. Lia passed through a stretch of native trees and introduced kiawe trees, past the hidden path to "her" surfing cove, and turned mauka into a gravel driveway through the trees that seemed to go nowhere. Not until you came out on the other side to acres of citrus—lemons, limes, oranges—and avocado trees, each variety separated by a row of banana plants.

As large as the farm was, it was only a fraction of the kuleana land dating back to the Great Mahele, when King Kamehameha III relinquished control over portions of the land, a right previously held by previous high chiefs and monarchs. It was the first time commoners could buy land, a concept previously alien to Hawaiian thinking. Over the years, pieces of the land had been sold off, often to pay attorneys to protect the family's interest in court from the developers who saw it only as lots for more mansions for North American owners, who seldom lived in them all year-round.

Greedy politicians, their palms greased by the same developers, had for decades used increased property taxes to force such families to sell or downsize, but recent changes in Maui's laws now protected native owners on the kuleana homesteads from such onerous tax burdens.

There was only the one pickup parked in front of the house. Lia knew Kāhea, one of Auntie Carol's granddaughters, recently divorced, was now living here with her three children, so she guessed maybe Kāhea had taken them to school or had maybe found a job.

Lia parked in the shade of one of the many large plumeria trees in the front of the house and could smell the heavy perfume of the blossoms before getting out of her pickup. She was immediately approached and sniffed by three large dogs; she reached back in for the bakery in the neat foil container, slammed the door and hollered, "Whooo-weee!" If the barking dogs hadn't alerted any occupants, maybe the traditional Hawaiian variation of "yoo-hoo" might.

Tiny Carol Kawaʻa, brown as a kukui nut and topped with short, snow-white hair, came out on the lānai and held the screen door open. "Aloha kaʻu kaikamahine! Howzit?"

Lia climb the steps to the lānai so the screen could be closed and bent her five-foot, ten-inch frame down to exchange honis with the respected five-two kupuna. "Maikaʻi loa, ʻanakē."

"Did you bring me banana bread?"

"ʻAʻole. Palaoa manakō."

"You made?"

Lia held up her hands, "ʻAe, with my own two not-so-little hands."

"You'll have a piece with me?"

"Sure. That way, if you don't like it, I can feed it to the dogs on the way out."

Auntie Carol scoffed. "Nonsense. I'm sure it's fine. You'll have some coffee?"

Lia's one grandmother had died when she was a baby, and the other had passed before Lia was born, so she never had a tūtū of her own and was happy she had found Auntie Carol, who treated her like one of her own many grandchildren.

They sat at the old formica kitchen table, getting caught up with each other's lives. Lia was as happy to hear it as Auntie was proud to tell it, but Kāhea had gotten a full-time job in beverage services at the Four Seasons resort. Her two oldest children, a boy and girl, were in the Hawaiian immersion school, and the youngest was napping in the family room, having fallen alseep watching a kids' program on 'Ōiwi TV.

"So, I hear you met my grandson, Kekoa?"

Lia smirked. She often stopped by to say "Hi." Was the reason for this visit so obvious?

"Yes, I did," she replied, smiling.

"Handsome, anei?" asked the kupunawahine, inserting the Hawaiian word that expected a "yes" or "no" answer.

"'Ae, he's very good-looking. Maika'i ho'i kō ia ala 'ōiwi kino, ho'i. *He has a nice build, too.*

"At *your* beach, I heard."

Lia laughed. "Of course, he told you about that! Did he ask if you had given me permission to cross your land?"

It was Auntie Carol's turn to chuckle. "Of course."

Now they both laughed.

"'Ono loa palaoa, Lia. Fresh, too. You just made?"

"Last night." She drank some more of her coffee and picked up the thread of their conversation.

"He seems very akamai, but needs to brush up on his Hawaiian history."

"'Ae," she answered, agreeing with both statements. "The price our people pay when they move to ka 'āina 'e," she said, inserting the Hawaiian slang for America. "They forget their mo'olelo.

"Did he tell you he graduated at the top of his class at university in San Diego? A degree in Criminal Justice."

"No, he never talks about himself unless I ask him a direct question."

The old woman gave a knowing smile. "It's OK, though, to be ha'aha'a, anei?"

Lia nodded in agreement. "I did find out he is a deputy sheriff."

"'Ae, a detective."

Lia's look of surprise told the auntie that this was news to her, but the kupuna read something else in the young woman's eyes.

The old woman took Lia's hand in hers, looked at her, and then nodded.

"He's found a place in your heart." A statement, not a question.

For some reason, tears welled up in her eyes. "I think I'm falling in love with him," she confessed. "How can that be? I've only known him six days."

"Who's to say, child? Where the pu'uwai is concerned, there is no explaining."

✦ ✦ ✦

CHAPTER 14

"**Y**OU'RE TELLING ME we've had three women murdered in as many weeks and no one—no one!—ever thought they might be connected?"

"Well, not until now, Chief," answered the assistant chief from the Criminal Division, giving side-eyes to the investigative captain and lieutenant.

"I'm surprised the mayor hasn't already called, especially with one of them being a tourist!"

"They were in different districts, Chief, so no one made the connection until the medical examiner brought it to our attention at the post."

"I know we're the second-biggest island, but Maui is only 48 by 26 miles. Do the districts make a point to compare notes on open cases, murders, at least?"

The police chief eyed the assistant chiefs, investigative captain, and his administrative captain for a moment, but the lack of an immediate response gave him the answer.

"OK, that ends today. Barry," he said, looking at his administrative captain, "draft a new policy. Once a week—pick a day—investigators from every district will meet via video feed and provide details on any open homicides to share information and see if there are any patterns.

"Now tell me about the cases," the chief said, looking at Lt. Dejillo.

"Last month, twenty-seven days ago, Misty Dawson, an approximate thirty-year-old known prostitute and meth addict, was found dead in an alley between buildings at the outlet in Lāhainā. Bruising on her neck indicated she had been strangled. She was naked from the waist down and obvious, fresh semen was found in her vaginal area. The thought was she had been raped and murdered."

"You got those details from the officer's report?"

"Yes, sir. We don't have the autopsy results yet."

"Doesn't that strike you as a bit conclusionary? How did the officer determine it was 'obvious' semen? Color, odor, viscosity, taste?"

"I guess it was an assumption, sir," replied the lieutenant, totally aware of the logical weakness of that response.

"Who discovered the body?"

"An employee from the magic show taking out trash the following morning. His supervisor called it in; details were relayed to Lāhainā station. They dispatched a unit, called out evidence techs, and alerted the M.E. Her purse with a fake ID—that's where the 'Misty Dawson' came from—and miscellaneous items, but no cash was found nearby."

"OK, brief the next one."

"Exactly two weeks later, the body of a homeless woman—"

The chief's head came up, and, before he could ask, the lieutenant said, "Which was determined by the layers of mismatched and dirty clothing and the shopping cart full of miscellaneous discards and trash near the body; so, it's unlikely she was killed somewhere else. She was found in a corner of the first level of the parking garage at the shopping center, likely where she was sleeping for the night. She, also, was naked from the waist down; her dirty underwear was found, torn, nearby. Again, the presence of *assumed* semen in the vaginal area indicated a likely rape. From ligature bruising on her neck, it was believed she had been strangled with a dirty silk scarf still around her neck."

Addressing both assistant chiefs, the chief said, "I know we don't have a dedicated homicide unit, but do we have any officers who have had any homicide training or maybe attended the National Homicide Investigators school?"

"I'll check," replied Barry Phipps, the administrative captain, who started texting on his electronic tablet. "Support Services Bureau maintains all the training records."

"Who rolled out on that one?" asked one of the assistant chiefs.

"A sector patrol unit and the shift sergeant. Extra units for security. The mall was just opening for the day."

"Who found the body?"

"An employee driving one of those miniature street sweepers alerted mall security. The body was under some stairs in a corner of the garage. It had been there for a while. Decomposition and animal activity on the corpse had already started. Therefore, time of death is an issue."

"So much for footprints, although I doubt any could be distinguished from any other," commented the chief as an aside.

"Chief, I just got a text from Phyllis," interjected Captain Phipps. "Sgt. Kalehuawehe was the last Maui officer to attend a homicide-related training class, a Blood Spatter Evidence course in Honolulu in 2018."

The chief was about to make a remark but decided it would be injudicious. "Tell me about the tourist."

Getting a nod to continue, the lieutenant went on. "HFD in Hāna received a call Sunday morning of an unresponsive woman in a pup tent at Waiʻānapanapa State Park. Other campers reported being awakened by the alarm on a cell phone going off for more than 30 minutes before another camper went over to complain. Getting no response, a man unzipped the door, and his wife shook the victim's foot, trying to get her to wake up. No response. Believing it was some kind of medical emergency, she called 911.

"A patrol unit from Hāna district was dispatched for crowd control. The paramedic determined the subject was deceased. The body was still in a lightweight sleeping bag. The responding officer, Finau Aholelei, made sure to take *in situ* photos with his phone before the bag was pulled out of the tent and more cell phone photos were taken. Fresh bruising that appeared to be from hands were evident on the neck. ID found in the tent identified the deceased as a Debra Caldwell, 21, from Elizabethtown, New Jersey.

"The medical examiner and Criminal Investigations Division were called. CID called the ME and agreed to wait for them at Pāʻia. Our unit—with flashing blue lights, no siren, and the ME van on its tail—it still took them more than an hour to get there, what with tourist traffic going to Hāna already in full swing."

"Two investigators from ISB arrived sometime thereafter," inserted the assistant chief of the Investigative Services Bureau, somewhat defensively. "It probably should have been our case from the start."

Before a turf war could start, the chief said, "No. CID keeps this case for now. If it is determined this really is the work of a serial killer, I'll decide who takes lead when the time comes."

The lieutenant continued his narrative. "Barrier tape had been put up early, that pissed off some of the campers whose cars or tents were inside the perimeter."

The chief shrugged his shoulders and emitted a huff, as if to say, "What else is new?"

"After the evidence techs got more photos, the ME unzipped the sleeping bag to move the deceased into a body bag, before she realized the victim was only wearing a t-shirt. Overheads on the fire truck and the police units had attracted the usual mob of onlookers, so the ME just moved the sleeping bag and contents into the body bag.

"Once SIS was satisfied they had all the photos they needed, the tent was taken down and brought back in their van.

"Notification has been made to the victim's family, but no relatives of the hooker and the homeless woman have been located yet."

"Thank you, Lieutenant." The chief scanned the room to make sure he had everyone's attention.

"This goes to the top of everyone's list, including Patrol. Unlikely the killer took a bus to Wai'ānapanapa. I want every vehicle with a light out, expired plate, too-dark window tint, outdated safety sticker and, of course, traffic violation, driven by a lone male to be stopped, ticketed, and a field interview card filled out. Support staff will upload the info off the cards as they come in."

"There's nothing to say the killer doesn't have a woman or child with him, boss," offered one of the assistant chiefs.

"True, but unlikely he's raping and killing women while his own woman waits in the car. We'll proceed on that assumption for now. And kid or kids? Unlikely at night, but again, not impossible."

+ + +

CHAPTER 15

CHIEF MAXWELL KORMAN dug his smartphone out of his pocket and went straight to the directory. Finding the correct name, he bypassed the office number and dialed his friend on his private phone.

Two decades ago, he and Gene Davis had gone through the San Diego Regional Police Academy together and climbed the ranks of law enforcement in their respective departments on similar tracks. However, Davis went higher and faster than Korman: deputy, investigator, sergeant, detective sergeant, lieutenant, captain, and commander before winning election as San Diego County Sheriff, even defeating his main challenger, the Undersheriff. The race was much tougher than Gene expected. But his campaign hammered on his experience at all levels of enforcement and investigative positions, incontrast to the sitting Undersheriff, the boss's heir apparent, who had served only in administrative positions nearly his entire career.

When the City Council passed over Assistant Chief Korman as the new chief for the San Diego Police Department, he started looking for other law-enforcement command opportunities. Then, almost miraculously—and giving credence to the notion that God doesn't close one door without opening another—a nationwide search went out for a new chief for the Maui Police Department. After a series of internal scandals, the Police Commission, at the urging of the County Council, decided it would consider new blood from outside the department, which had traditionally promoted from within.

He didn't know if it helped, but surely it didn't hurt that his wife was born on Oʻahu and that she and their daughter danced with a hula hālau in San Diego. He had once been a racer in one of the several outrigger canoe clubs in the county, so he wasn't totally ignorant of the culture.

Korman was ninety-five percent sure this was a serial killer. He had given this call a lot of thought, going back and forth on its wisdom. *Not to decide is to decide*, he reminded himself and thumbed the number in the screen.

"Max, how are you? Yeah, yeah, I know. You're in Hawaiʻi—how could anything be the matter?" he kidded.

Max gave an obligatory chuckle and said, "Not everything's perfect in paradise, Gene. That's why I'm calling.

"We have murders here, of course, but they're often crimes of passion with obvious suspects or armed robberies gone bad that my criminal-investigation unit solves pretty quickly. But murders aren't so commonplace or numerous that the department ever needed a dedicated homicide unit."

"Yeah, so why are you calling me? You want a list of our homicide protocols?"

"Funny, Gene. I ran a 187 team, remember? I've wrestled with this a day and a night, and it's going to piss off a lot of my own guys, but I wonder if you can spare an experienced homicide investigator and send him, or her, assigned TDY to me. But I'm getting ahead of myself.

"I've got a likely serial killer running around my island. The latest vic was a young female tourist, and the media and certain council members, particularly the ones who wanted a local for my job, are out to lynch me. Tourism is one of our primary industries on Maui. And if that wasn't enough, I have my first annual review coming up before the Police Commission.

"None of my guys are trained homicide investigators. As far as I know, none of them belong to the National Homicide Investigators Association and I'm sure none has ever gone to the NHIA school."

Davis almost said, "Whose fault is that?" but Korman beat him to the punch. "Yeah, I know, that's on me.

"On top of that, I don't have a crime lab. The only one in the state is in Honolulu."

"Max, my friend, you are going to owe me *so* big on this. I'm already thinking of an all-expense trip for two to Maui. OK, I'll lend you one of my guys. Not the most experienced but a real go-getter. He stumbled across a stiff while on patrol, called out detectives, put up barrier tape, and then started marking likely evidence he had already located. A cigarette butt, blood drops, some footprints, I forget all what else. He didn't have any of those little tent markers the evidence techs use, so he put road flares from his trunk to mark the locations. When backup arrived, he left that deputy on the barrier and started walking up and down the block looking for all the houses that had security cameras. It turned out to all be crucial evidence; he had the case half-solved before the dicks got there. And two of those home security cameras got good profiles of the killer.

"The homicide lieutenant was so impressed, he says initiative like that needs to be rewarded. Told the detective sergeant to send the kid to the next NHIA conference and then add him to his team when he got back."

"Sounds great. So is that who you're going to send me?"

"Oh, no, Max. I'm not going to send him." Pause. "He's already there! While you were talking, I was emailing his lieutenant and found out something else that, I guess, might help. He grew up on Maui, so he'll know his way around."

Chief Korman could not believe his good luck. "You're right, Gene. I'm going to owe you big time."

Sheriff Davis laughed. "You already do, buddy!

"I'll have his lieutenant call him forthwith."

+ + +

CHAPTER 16

JUSTIN WAS LYING in bed, stretching, waiting for his usual morning erection to go down so he could go pee. He could tell the sun was just coming up. He had transitioned his body clock to Hawai'i time within 48 hours of arrival. Roosters crowed outside somewhere, and the monotonous call of a francolin seem to go on forever. They were another example of an introduced species run amok, like cattle egrets and axis deer.

His first thought was the great time he'd had with Lia the previous night. When that mind-video finished, he began wondering how he would spend the day. At the top of his agenda was to go on another date with Lia. She had said that she had to open the store today, so he suspected she was probably already at the coffee shop or on her way. Best not to call her at work, but a quick text would do.

His phone, kept under his pillow for security and privacy, started ringing next to his head. His first thought was she beat him to it but was disappointed when he saw the 619 area code—recognizing it as the main number from Imperial Beach Station, *his* station.

"Hello?"

"Deputy Opio?"

"Yes, this is he."

"This is Lt. Ordeñas."

"Yes, sir?"

"I just got a call from headquarters, from *the* Undersheriff."

I bet that doesn't happen very often, like never!

"You've been detailed for temporary duty to the Maui Police Department. Report to the Criminal Investigations Division at 0700 tomorrow. It's a plainclothes assignment. Do you have a sidearm with you?"

"Yes, sir." *More than one, actually.*

"Wear it."

"How long will I be here, sir?"

"Unknown. Until you receive further orders from me or someone higher in command, the Sheriff's Office will continue to cover your salary, benefits, vacation accrual, et cetera. Any miscellaneous expenses will be reimbursed with the appropriate voucher.

"Any questions?"

"Any idea what this is about, sir?"

"Not a clue. Anything else?"

"No, sir. Not at this time."

"Have fun. Consider it a working vacation."

WELL, HE KNEW how part of his day would be spent. He'd have to get some more clothes. He thought about all the great law-enforcement sport shirts he had at home. Plenty of pants, too. *Oh, well. There's a TJ Maxx and a Ross in Kahului. I wonder if I can voucher it as a legit travel expense?*

He got up, deodorized, washed his face, swished with mouthwash, and brushed his teeth. He had shaved yesterday evening and knew he could get by without shaving this morning. One of the advantages of being Hawaiian: light beard. He put on shorts, a MauiBuilt T-shirt, and slippers, and was ready for breakfast. Back to the Tasty Crust Restaurant for a repeat of yesterday.

While he waited for his food, he scanned a *Maui News* someone had left behind. It seemed pretty thin on news, but he did read an article about a New Jersey girl found dead in her tent at Wai'ānapanapa two days earlier. Foul play was suspected. The lack of details made him suspect the police were keeping a lid on information getting out.

He took another drink of his coffee and pulled out his phone.

Good morning, lovely. Something has come up. Good news, I think. I want to tell you in person. I think you said you were on till 6 and I told my aunt I'd be home for dinner and you have practice tonight so it might have to wait until tomorrow.

✦ ✦ ✦

CHAPTER 17

THE 'ĪAO VALLEY was still in a cloud when Kekoa left his aunt and uncle's house for his first day at the new assignment. It was 0545, and he figured that would give him enough time to get breakfast at Tasty Crust and still get to police headquarters before seven.

He turned off Mahalani into the driveway under the wide monkeypod canopy and followed other cars into the Employees Only lot. Without a key or pass code, he hurried to go through the back door with a woman carrying her purse and a shopping bag from which a gift-wrapped box peeked out.

"Someone have a baby?"

"Yes, Detective Chang, you know, Anastasia. It's her first day back from maternity leave. I got her a 'twosie.' People always get newborn sizes but never anything for the baby to grow into."

"Sorry, I don't know her," interjected Kekoa before this lesson on infant wear went much further. "It's my first day on a temporary transfer from the sheriff's office." He decided prefixing it with "San Diego" might be too confusing or raise unnecessary questions. "Can you direct me to the Investigations Division?"

"That's where Anastasia and I work. Just follow me. "I'm Lucy Ortiz, by the way."

"Aloha kakahiaka, Lucy. I'm Justin Opio, but most people use my middle name, Kekoa."

"Well, welcome aboard, Kekoa."

Kekoa followed the woman through a few hallways and then hurried ahead to open the door into Investigations for her. Inside, he saw the typical arrangement of pairs of facing desks throughout the room, except for individual cubicles, where clerical staff was starting to arrive.

"I'm supposed to see Lt. Dayrit. Can you point out his office?"

Lucy had just finished putting her purse in a bottom drawer of her deck and was sliding it closed. "Over there by the windows. Can you see his door?"

"I do now. Mahalo."

Kekoa took a seat on a plastic chair outside the lieutenant's office and underwent the expected eyeballing by the detectives as they wandered in. For his first day, Kekoa thought it best to wear a sport jacket, not knowing what the usual mufti was for detectives at MPD. His coat was unbuttoned, and he could tell some of the ever-vigilant dicks had made him as a cop, if not necessarily from his badge or the pistol alongside it. He saw most of them wore short-sleeved or polo shirts, and only a few had dress shirts and ties but not jackets.

One of the arriving detectives spied him from the door, did a quick head shake, and walked right over.

"Kekoa! What are you doing here?" he asked, extending his hand. Kekoa had risen to his feet as soon as they made eye contact and met the hearty handclasp, neither one trying to push a "man hug."

"Good to see you, Kaloli'i. I didn't know you went into police work, much less made detective," he kidded. They both knew all the other investigators were paying attention to their greeting and heard a few muffled chuckles from the room.

"Yeah, got my AA in Criminal Justice at Maui College; I had no intention of going for a Bachelor's, so I came over here." Then pushing open the right side of Kekoa's jacket, "And you're strapped, too! Are you the new guy we were told to expect?"

"I expect so," grinned Kekoa.

Kekoa and Kaloli'i sensed the mood in the room shift and turned to see an older man exuding "command presence" coming down the aisle by the windows.

"Here's the lieutenant now," announced Kaloli'i, turning and threading his way through the desks to his own. Kekoa remained standing.

"You Opio?" asked the lieutenant as he turned into his office. "Come in," he said before Kekoa could answer. "Have a seat," he added without bothering with a handshake.

From his size and coloring, Kekoa took him as being of Filipino descent. When the lieutenant turned his back to remove his sport coat, put it on a wood hanger, and hang it on a coat tree, Kekoa scanned the room. The usual wall of awards and training certificates, photos of the lieutenant and various dignitaries, a photo of the wife and kids in a clear-plastic display frame on the desk.

Then, whether an afterthought or intentionally delayed, the lieutenant reached across the desk with an extended hand, which Kekoa met and shook.

"I'm Oscar Dayrit, the lieutenant of the Criminal Investigations Unit. The division also has a captain and an assistant chief—they're upstairs on mahogany row—both of whom are taking heat from the chief on this suspected serial killer, which, of course, is rolling downhill on yours truly.

"So, you're some hotshot murder cop from the Mainland who's going to show us how to run this investigation?" His tone made it clear that Kekoa wasn't exactly welcome. *Damn. What did my command staff get me into?*

"Listen, Loo, before we get off on the wrong foot, this is all news to me. I didn't ask for this, and this is the first I'm learning why I'm here. I was here visiting family when my lieutenant said our boss, the undersheriff, called him and ordered me here as a temporary duty assignment. As for murders, I don't claim to be any expert. I had some luck with my first homicide investigation, but they were impressed enough to transfer me to one of our Homicide teams and send me to the National Homicide Investigations training conference. I'm not here to get in the way or make anyone look bad."

The two men were looking each other in the eye during that entire little speech.

"Fair enough, Opio. I'll be honest; no one made this as a serial until the chief suggested it. Three different victims in different parts of the island, nothing in common as far as age, race, or lifestyle."

"OK, show me what you have, and I'll see if there's anything that jumps out at me. Sometimes fresh eyes help. Can I meet the other guys on the team?"

"Everyone is out there in the squad bay, and I'll take you around when we get back. First, the chief wants to meet you."

They left Investigations and went down some halls and up an elevator until they reached the office with "Chief of Police" in raised letters on a brass plate next to the door. A large anteroom housed two administrative staff, a couch, and some chairs. One of the women, most likely the chief's secretary, said, "He's expecting you. Go on in."

The lieutenant knocked once and opened the door without waiting for a reply.

"Good morning, chief. I'd like you to meet Deputy Opio from the San Diego Sheriff's Office."

The chief came around from behind his desk to greet the newcomer, examining the visitor. After a handshake, he invited Kekoa to take one of the chairs in front of his desk, and he took the other one, turning it to face Kekoa. The lieutenant was relegated to a chair against the wall near the door.

"I apologize for interrupting your vacation, Deputy—do you mind if I call you Justin?—but when I asked your boss for one of his hotshot homicide investigators, he told me you were already on the island!

"Did you know Gene and I went to the regional police academy together?"

"No, sir, I did not know that. As to the vacation, I'll make sure they extend me on the other end." He gave a weak chuckle. "Also, 'Justin' is fine, but, if you didn't know, I was born and raised in Wailuku, and most people here call me by middle name, Kekoa. So, whichever you're comfortable with."

"Great. If you're good with Kekoa, that's what we'll call you.

"Oscar or the investigators can bring you up to date on the case, but, basically, we had a hooker killed in Lāhaina, a bag lady at the shopping mall, and a camper down near Hāna in less than four weeks. Sheriff Davis told me you just graduated from the National Homicide Investigators five-day school, and I'm hoping you may have some ideas we've missed or direction we should take.

"We don't have a lot of murders in Maui County. The ones that do occur, we have a likely suspect determined pretty quickly and arrests not long after that. Consequently, there is no dedicated homicide unit or anyone with your training. The guys have been told you were coming and to work with you but, as you might imagine, there might be a sense of animosity of a stranger barging in on their case, so don't let them scare you off.

"Comments or questions, so far?"

Kekoa didn't like that the lieutenant was being left out of the conversation up till now and turned to include him in his next remark. "I got the impression that the work is spread out throughout the Investigations Division. Is that right?"

"Pretty much," said Lt. Dayrit.

"Rather than take investigators away from their other cases, I wonder if it might be possible for you to pick two, three, or four whose primary focus could just be on these murders for now?"

"Oscar?"

The lieutenant shrugged. "Let me give it some thought. It's not a bad idea."

"Anything else?"

"Unless you have already, is there a conference room or other area away from other foot traffic and other distractions, where the homicide investigators can set up shop? Also, I didn't see any in the squad room, but some portable display boards, either cork or whiteboard, for posting photos, notes, et cetera can be handy. Oh, yeah—I'll need some body armor."

The chief looked at the lieutenant, who didn't seem to be opposed to the idea. "Done," he said, and then laughed. "The clerical staff may not like giving up their party room."

The chief's desk phone rang. "Well, get started on those moves and, Oscar, keep me updated. Say, an email synopsis every Friday unless something new breaks?"

"10–4, chief," he replied.

✦ ✦ ✦

CHAPTER 18

THE LIEUTENANT LED Kekoa downstairs and down two halls to the aforementioned conference room. Kekoa saw it already had three six-foot folding tables.

"This would be perfect, Loo. Are there computer outlets?"

"The whole building is on WiFi. I'll decide who's coming over here shortly. They can bring their own desk chairs and computers until I get Facilities to move five desks in here. I'll get you some of the portable bulletin boards. Later, we'll go have the armorer find a new vest your size.

"Let's go introduce you to the team."

When they re-entered the Investigations room, the lieutenant shouted "Hey!" and when he had everyone's attention, he said, "This is Detective Kekoa Opio, a homicide investigator from San Diego Sheriff's. He grew up on Maui and has been detailed over to MPD to assist with this possible serial killer. Make him welcome."

Kekoa walked further into the room, and most of the men and women all came forward to introduce themselves and welcome him, although it seemed a bit chilly with a few of them. Some of the ones at nearby desks didn't bother coming over and just waved or nodded from where they sat or stood. Others asked questions about how long he had been a deputy, when he had left Maui, and, in typical Hawaiian style, questions about his family tree to see if there was any familial connections on one of the branches.

A short time later, Lt. Dayrit came out of his office, and the room quieted down.

"Listen up! In alphabetical order, Chang, Crane, and Ferko are assigned to the triple-murder investigation. Chang, you'll take the lead. Grab your chairs, laptops, homicide notes, and anything else you need from your desk right now, and move to the conference room down the hall. Anyone else with crime-scene notes or photos, give them to Opio. He'll see you later with other questions.

"Jocelyn," he said, addressing one of the unit secretaries, "You'll go over as clerical support. Use those tables until I get you desks in there. Oh, and send out an email that Anastasia's party is moved to the cafeteria."

Kekoa watched them start gathering their things to reaffirm he knew who each was. He soon learned their biographies.

Anastasia Chang didn't look Asian, so maybe it was a married name. She was about five-foot-four and the first out the door, reminding everyone who was the designated lead.

Roger Crane was the oldest, a Nebraska native, and stood about an inch taller than Keokoa's six-foot-one. He said he stayed in Hawai'i after twenty years with the Marine Corps because his Japanese-American wife was from O'ahu and didn't want to leave the Islands. They relocated here for the job.

As they moved down the hall, he leaned over to Kekoa, nodded his chin to Detective Chang up ahead, and whispered, "Don't let her size fool you. She's a champion kick-boxer."

Bobby Ferko was the youngest in the group. Kekoa made him for early- to mid-twenties, young for a detective, but who was he to talk! Although he knew a couple of Ferkos in San Diego, they were of Croatian ancestry, and Bobby definitely looked like he was a good part Filipino. Such was the genetic melting pot of Hawai'i.

Once they were in the conference room, they all looked to him, including Detective Chang, so he jumped right in.

"Once again, I'm Kekoa Opio. My haole name is Justin, in case you were interested. I did get to attend the National Homicide Investigators training conference not long ago and picked up a few ideas that you may already know and, if not, I am happy to share with you.

"I've asked the lieutenant to get us some display boards so we can pin up or paste up all the crime-scene photos. If they're up there every day, we're more apt to look at them from time to time, and maybe something we didn't see in an earlier view will jump out at us. If nothing else, it should keep us pissed off and motivated to get this guy.

"Until we get those boards, let's put the photos from each crime scene on a separate table in the order they occurred and then, Anastasia, could you bring me up to date on each murder?"

"Call me 'Stays.'"

"Pardon me."

"Everyone here calls me 'Stays.' I don't like 'Ana,' so 'Stays' is the next part of my name. One syllable is quicker than five."

"Got it."

Bobby had to go back and get the bag-lady photos from another detective; once all three tables were covered,

Stays began. She proved she was very familiar with the facts of each case, and the other detectives moved along with her from one table to the next.

When she was finished, Kekoa looked at them and said, "I would definitely call this the work of the same person, so, yes, you have a serial rapist killer on the loose.

"Most serial killers are narcissists. They have no empathy for others, and victims are just there for them to use and discard. When they do something that might be considered kind, it is not because they are being charitable but simply to make themselves feel good about themselves and how above others they are.

"All three women were raped and strangled, but notice how each body is staged the same way. Look how he has placed the vic's hands, palms down, over their face. My guess is he didn't want these women 'looking' at him, accusing him. The perp had to have rezipped the sleeping bag after the latest murder, but notice how he zipped it to hold her forearms to keep the hands over the face. It also shows he's methodical and didn't feel rushed."

"Maybe because he was out of view in the tent," suggested Anastasia.

"Yep, good thinking," responded Kekoa.

"But not the second one," observed Roger. "Her hands are over her ears. Maybe a 'see no evil, hear no evil' scenario?"

"Certainly a possibility, but I think more likely gravity or the effects of rigor pulled her arms away enough to reveal the face. And notice how the palms are still turned down, more in a 'peek-a-boo' formation and not as if they had been covering her ears."

No one commented, but neither did anyone disagree.

"So, tell me about the first victim. Who was she, where was she from, how old was she, et cetera?"

Detective Crane referred to some notes. "She was a prostitute who generally worked in Lāhainā. Her purse and wallet were found near the body. Any money had been stolen. The ID in her wallet was fake. Beat cops and any people who spoke to her more than once only knew her by various street names. No known relatives, and no one has come forward asking about her. If she had a cell phone, none was found. The ME puts her age in the middle to late twenties, although she looks older without the makeup. Her tox was positive for meth, so she was probably hooking to support her habit."

"Time of death?" asked Kekoa.

"The ME puts it between 10 p.m. and 2 a.m. The body wasn't found until the following morning. That's a popular parking lot, but the Front Street supper crowd was over by ten, and the magic show had already let out; they had only one performance that night. Bars were still open but none nearby, although there's an all-night McDonald's close, but they have their own parking lot."

"How did the killer get there, and how did he leave? It might be likely he had his own vehicle, but we can't assume he did, right?"

The others all agreed.

"What about DNA?" Kekoa asked. The others all chuckled.

"Even though most hookers douche after each john . . ." began Roger.

"No one likes riding another guy's wet deck," interjected Bobby. Kekoa glanced over at Anastasia, who shook her head and rolled her eyes.

Roger continued, "The ME said there were sperm cells from at least three men in her vagina and more in her underwear, which was found nearby. The prosecutor will call it 'built-in reasonable doubt.'"

"Bobby, will you be our scribe this morning and start taking notes?" Kekoa asked.

"Sure. Fire away."

"We want to put together a list of things Patrol can help with. I'm not familiar with your chain of command yet, but I suppose the Investigations captain will have to talk to their captain. First, Lāhainā division needs to scour a two-block radius of the crime scene for all security cameras and get copies of disks or tapes from that night. If that doesn't turn up anything, they'll need to go door-to-door looking for home security cameras, including the doorbell cameras. I got a good profile of my killer on one of those Ring cameras.

"Videos like that don't just help with ID but can also help establish a timeline. One of the perp running from the crime scene can help the prosecutor argue consciousness of guilt."

"Have them brace any other hookers in the area. They usually all know each other. See if anyone had her phone number. If we get that, we can try calling it, see if the killer answers, and triangulate a location off the cell towers." He saw two of his new partners look at each other and raise their eyebrows. Evidently no one had thought of that.

"Jocelyn, can you get us three of those big three-ring binders? I think they're three or three-and-half inches wide, and two or three boxes of those clear-plastic slip sheets for our murder books?"

Kekoa didn't want to embarrass anyone and ask if they used murder books here, so he just acted like they did. A murder book provided a uniform structure in one repository of all the police reports, lab reports, photos, drawings, property-room tags, and other materials involved in a homicide investigation, for others—whether other detectives, supervisors, or prosecutors—to review and locate key investigative information. It also ensured proper documentation of a homicide to support a cold-case investigation if it came to that.

"Do any of you know if the evidence technicians found any trace evidence?" Kekoa asked.

"I'm sure they've looked," answered Anastasia. "Strange, but did anyone notice that all three vics have their tops on? Maybe tits didn't do it for this guy, but it may help with trace-evidence transfer. I'm not expecting much from the alley scene, and the bag lady was living in a dirty environment, but the tourist tent should be a goldmine."

"Where's the sleeping bag and tent now?" Kekoa wanted to know.

"Another detective had the evidence techs set up in one of the garage bays."

"We should all go down and examine it at some point."

THE FACILITIES PEOPLE didn't move the five desks into the conference room until late in the day. Jocelyn, the administrative assistant, set up her desk promptly and then went to Supply to get office supplies for her and the four detectives. The three MPD personnel did not want to move everything from their desks in the Investigations room, so she came back with a Georgia Pacific paper box filled with enough pens—ballpoint and felt tip—pencils, tablets, staplers, rulers, scissors, tape, and tape dispensers for everyone. Kekoa was just happy to have a desk.

"The lieutenant said landline phones will be installed for each desk tomorrow and make do with our cells in the meantime. See you then." She pushed in her chair, picked up her purse, and left for the day.

Bobby said, "Let's help Stays carry all her baby loot out to her car before we go 10–9."

✦ ✦ ✦

CHAPTER 19

"I WONDER WHAT got kumu in a mood tonight? 'You have to be solid on the basics!'" mimicked Miki'ala in their teacher's voice.

"She was sure upset about something. Making us do beginner moves over and over and over again. I didn't see anyone messing up in the mirror. Did you?"

"No, except me, toward the end. I could barely hold my arms up."

"My legs are still quivering."

"Hey, what's going on up there?"

Lia and Miki'ala were coming home from hula practice when they saw a psychedelic display of flashing blue and blinking white lights up ahead.

"It must be a major pile-up to require that many police cars."

"Yeah, but if it's an accident, wouldn't there be a fire truck there?"

As they got closer, they saw flares on the highway reducing traffic down to one lane and an officer with a red flashlight additionally signaling people over and slowing them down. Other officers were walking slowly along the shoulder in both directions and others up on a rise, heads down, and sweeping the ground with their flashlights.

Lia's truck was creeping past the area, but no wreck could be seen. They saw something lying in the grass above the shoulder and people without uniforms standing near it and talking while a camera flashed multiple times.

"Lia, look!" shouted Miki'ala, pointing. "It's Kekoa!"

After checking traffic to make sure it was safe, Lia turned her head, and her jaw dropped. It was Kekoa! Wearing khaki slacks and a dark sport shirt, with a badge on his belt next to a holster. He had a gun!

As she resumed driving, with Miki still gawking out the passenger window, which she had since rolled down, Lia wondered why she was so shocked. He had told her he was a deputy sheriff, and Auntie Carol said he was a detective, but why was he working here? On Maui!

"I wonder what's going on?" Miki'ala wondered aloud. "Didn't that look like a body on the ground where those guys were standing? Maybe it was a hit and run.

"You said he texted you today and said he had something to tell you. Maybe it had something to do with that thing on the highway?"

Lia had been wondering, also, if the text was connected to this—which certainly seemed to be a crime scene.

"Yeah, maybe," she finally answered.

"Was he carrying a gun when you went to dinner?" asked Miki'ala, even more curious.

"I don't know. He *is* a cop. I never thought about it. He was wearing a sport coat," replied Lia, who was thinking about it now. *Maybe I need to know more about this guy before I get in too deep.*

IT WAS AFTER 11, but he decided to call anyway; he needed to tell her. The phone rang three times before she answered.

"Did I wake you up?"

"No, I was just getting into bed."

"Remember when I said I had something to tell you? Well, this is it. I wanted to share the good news—at least I thought it would be—in person, but the day got all used up.

"What I wanted to tell you was my department has loaned me to MPD to help with this serial-killer case. *Please* do *not* share that with anyone! The news media will start connecting the killings soon enough. We want to keep them from getting in the way as long as we can."

She noticed the plural pronouns and how he already considered himself part of the county police. "This guy is sick, and we're not sure we've accounted for all the victims yet."

"Miki'ala and I saw you along the highway tonight. Was that part of your case?"

"No, thank goodness. Unrelated murder.

"Anyway, this assignment might mean we can see each other a bit more if you're up for that."

"Sure." *I wish you were here now.*

"The downside is it might mean late nights if this guy keeps going." He heard her yawn. "I'm sorry for calling so late. I should let you go."

"No, I'm usually up reading or studying until midnight, but our kumu hula really worked us hard tonight."

"That's where you were coming from?"

"Yeah."

"If I can get loose, can I take you to lunch tomorrow?"

"Sure, but I get to pick the place."

"Deal. Good night, Lia."

"Good night, Kekoa. Call me in the morning if you can."

+ + +

CHAPTER 20

KEKOA HAD PUT Lia's number in his Contacts as soon as he got it, so he smiled when his phone rang and her name appeared on the screen. He pushed the button to receive, but before he could say a word, she asked, "Are you free tonight?"

"Yes."

"Come down here, and I'll take you to dinner."

"What time?

"At least a half hour before sunset, if not sooner, and dress casually, like shorts and slippers."

"Okay," he replied, wondering what she had planned.

When he got there, he parked on the shoulder alongside the wall, like the time they went out to dinner, and was happy the space wasn't taken. Her truck was in the spot next to her lānai, and he saw lights on in her landlord's house further back on the property.

She opened the door after his first knock. He was wearing shorts and an aloha shirt. She was wearing cutoffs and a tank top over a sport bra. They kissed hello.

"Perfect timing. Here, you carry this," handing him a folded blanket. She put one strap of a backpack over one shoulder and gently backed him up so she could pull the door shut. "Let's go."

"Well, first put these in the house. Tomatoes from my aunt's garden."

"Yum! Mahalo."

He followed her out of the yard, and, when she got to the sidewalk, she turned and smiled. "We're going to the beach for the sunset."

"Sounds good to me."

They started walking side by side down her block to the ocean that could be seen on her entire street. After two or three steps, he took her hand. She looked at him, smiled, and gave his hand a little squeeze. They both realized it was the first time they had held hands, and how well their hands fit together.

They walked around the barrier at the end of the street and out onto the sand. It was her plan, so he let her decide where they would put down the blanket, which turned out to be a hike farther down the beach, away from any other sunset-watchers. After spreading out the blanket, they kicked off their slippers and sat down.

The afternoon wind had picked up, so the sea was slightly choppy with occasional whitecaps. The shore break was mild and not too loud.

"I'm glad you were free. And your damn phone better not go off. I should have told you to leave it at the house."

He laughed. "Yeah, get me in trouble with the new lieutenant the first week."

She pushed him back onto the blanket. "Shut up and kiss me."

They engaged in some playful necking and he felt her unbuttoning his shirt. "What are you doing?"

"I want to look at your chest. I like your brown skin. Is that so bad?" she replied and ran her open hand slowly over his torso.

"No, it feels nice." *It's also giving me a hard-on.*

He sat up while he still could. "So, what's in the backpack?"

She reached over, unzipped the top compartment, and extracted a bottle of wine.

"Keep it down here on the blanket when we're not drinking from it. You know glass is not allowed on the beach. I've never seen any enforcement down here, but it's best *you* don't get a ticket," she said with a grin. She twisted off the cap, took a swallow, and handed him the bottle.

He took a swig and looked at the label. "White zinfandel."

"Yeah, nothing fancy. Kind of Kool-Aid with a kick."

He laughed at the apt description and took another swallow. "Clear horizon. We might see the Green Flash."

"Maybe. Another 15 minutes," she said and lifted the bottle.

They watched the sparkling path of light from the sun to the shore dancing on the waves before they both saw the Green Flash. The orange glow from the sun beneath the horizon gradually grew dimmer before she pulled them down on the blanket next to the empty bottle.

"Oh, so that was your plan—get me half-toasted and take advantage of me," he teased.

"Shucks, you figured me out already!" They kissed for a while, both enjoying the mellow buzz from the wine, and just lay there, cuddling for a while.

"I'm sorry," he said, when they both heard his stomach growl.

"Don't be. That's our signal to go. Dinner awaits."

After shaking out and folding the blanket, they walked hand in hand again the block and a half to her place. They stepped out of their slippers on the lānai and entered her cottage, or ʻohana, as it's known in Hawaiʻi. It was the first time he had been inside. The door opened to the tiny kitchen. A small table and two chairs were against the wall to the right. Farther away to the left, by the window, was a couch with two end tables featuring mismatched lamps. Down the short hallway, he could see the bedroom and a door on the right he assumed was the bathroom.

"This is my home."

"Nice. Very cozy."

"My landlords are great, haven't ever raised my rent. I clean their chicken coop out back and occasionally feed, and I think they're afraid to lose me." She laughed. "And they let me have fresh eggs whenever I want.

"I hope you like spaghetti. Sauce from a jar, but I add pork sausage and other personal touches."

He watched as she tied her long hair into a knot on the top of her head; then she turned on the oven and two burners on the electric stove. "I had already preheated the oven and turned off the sauce and water when you got here, so it won't take long to heat them up again. Would you get the wine out of the fridge?"

"Sure. Just warning you, I'm not much of a drinker. Usually two beers and I'm out."

"Quit whining and pour."

"Oh, a real cork this time! Where's your corkscrew?"

She shifted her butt to the left as she was breaking up the pasta into the boiling water. "That drawer there."

"Was that one of your hula moves?"

"Absolutely," she said, looking over her shoulder and grinning at him. He watched her put frozen garlic bread on a baking sheet and shove it in the oven. She gave each pan a stir and took a half step to the refrigerator, got out a half-gallon bottle of water, and filled the glasses on the table next to the stemless wine glasses.

It surprised him how much he enjoyed watching her work. He had never paid attention at the coffee shop, nor was he there long enough anyhow, but he was impressed by her seemingly effortless efficiency. The fact that she was such a striking beauty was worth watching, too.

KEKOA WIPED HIS mouth with his paper napkin. "That was great, Lia. Your personal touches to the sauce, whatever they were, were outstanding. I'm stuffed."

"Nahh, there's always room for dessert." She removed two pie plates from the fridge on which slices of what looked like banana bread were already cut. "It's okay if you can't finish it, but at least try a bite."

"Yum! But that's not banana bread . . ."

"Didn't say it was, smartie."

"Mango!"

She smiled. "No wonder they made you a detective."

He grinned across the table at her joke. "This is really good! Yeah, maybe I do have room for the whole slice."

When he finished, she took his hand. "Let's sit on the couch. I'll clean this up later. Bring your wine glass." On the way, she touched the wall switch and turned off the overhead light in the kitchen.

"This is my living room, four steps from the kitchen. It's a foldout couch if anyone stays over." He watched her put her glass on an end table, twist the rod to close the bamboo blinds, and turn down the lamp. "There's reflective tinting on that window to help keep out some of the heat, but no one can see in."

She took a drink of her wine, and he mimicked her action. "Do you mind me asking you about your work?"

"Not at all. Just understand, I can only tell you things about this investigation that've already been made public."

"Okay."

"Anything in particular you want to know?"

"Are you armed right now?"

He laughed out loud. It wasn't what he was expecting. He patted his shorts and said, "Pocket knife."

"What about when we went to dinner?"

"I was. An ankle gun. You might recall I hardly rolled up my pants leg and stayed away from the water when we walked on the beach.

"Now that you know that I sometimes have a gun on me, there's something important I need to tell you if we're going to keep seeing each other . . ."

She suddenly sat up straight. "*If?* You mean you don't think we are? Or are you already giving yourself an 'out'?"

He was startled by the shocked look in her face. "No! No, that's not what I meant. Yes, I want to keep seeing you. I want us to be together, and that's why I have to tell you this for both our safety."

"Now you're scaring me a different way."

"Just listen. If we ever get caught in a man-with-a-gun situation, a robbery or a carjacking, for example, don't *ever* say, 'You have a gun, do something.' A cop's wife got him killed by saying that during a holdup. *I'll* be the one to decide to get involved *or not.* Understand?"

"Yes," she answered, but she was suddenly frightened by this violent potential in him, who had seemed so gentle up until now.

"Don't worry. You know there's not a lot of shootings on Maui . . ."

"Are you fooling? They're on the news more and more here. Some guy got shot on the Mokulele Highway a while back."

He took her closest hand and pulled her down to his shoulder. "We're fine. I'm not going anywhere," he said as he stroked her hair.

"You have really thick hair compared to most blondes I've known."

"I won't ask how many that's been, but it's not true blonde, you know, just sun-bleached right now from surfing. I'm really a dishwater blonde, kind of a light sandy-brown."

He was still running his fingers through it. "I like long hair. It looks good on you."

"It's taking me forever to get it grown out to this length. It falls just to my waist."

"I know. I've noticed when you've had it down," he said, grinning.

"Some of my hula sisters have never had their hair cut. Some have it to the bottoms of their butts."

"Miki'ala?"

"'A'ole. She shortened it once in high school—for some guy. Stupid."

"Are you the only blonde in your hālau?"

"Dishwater, but yes."

"I've see one or two blondes on TV at Merrie Monarch. They really stand out."

"And I always wonder if the judges are watching them more closely. And if I ever get there, I'll be a full head or taller than anyone else."

He reached for his glass on the end table, swallowed the last of his wine, turned off the lamp, and kissed her. Before long, they were lying face to face on the couch, necking. After a while, she pulled her face back to look at him, "Do you think I'm pretty?"

He snorted. "Of course, I do. I think you're beautiful."

"And you're obviously attracted to me."

"Isn't this proof of that?"

"Yeah. I know it's only like the third time, but this is all we ever do." She saw the quizzical look on his face. "Like tonight at the beach, you seemed to like it when I was touching your chest."

"I did."

"Then when we were necking on the blanket, no one was around; don't you think I might have liked to be touched, too? You could have at least copped a feel if you wanted—I wouldn't have stopped you—but you never try anything or even ask me if I want to."

"And what would you think if I shoved my hand into your pants right now?" She didn't answer. "You know why I don't? Because I don't want to screw this up by pushing too fast or too hard." He paused and stroked her hair again. "I like you, Lia. You're a smart, clever, funny woman, and you must be patient if you teach grade-school kids. Your beauty is just frosting on the cake. I watched you in the kitchen tonight, how smooth and efficiently you do everything; I suspect you're like that all the time and I couldn't help but be even more impressed with you. And I can't wait to see you dance.

"Yes, Lia, I'm more than attracted to you. I'm falling in love with you . . ."

She took his face in her hands, kissed him chastely on the lips, stood up, took his hand, and led him down the hall.

+ + +

CHAPTER 21

LIA LOOKED DOWN, admiring his strong, brown back and top of his butt before the sheet began. *Oops, sorry about those scratch marks.* She leaned over and licked his ear. When he stirred, she whispered, "Time to get up, sleepy-head."

He opened his eyes. "It's still dark. What time is it?"

"Five. You have to go home and change before work."

"You're already up," he declared but watched as she pulled a t-shirt over her well-tanned torso and wiggled out of her cutoffs.

"Slide over. We have some unfinished business, but first swish with this and swallow it. Oranges from the neighbor's tree and fresh squeezed this morning."

"You know you're spoiling me."

"You ain't seen anything yet, fella."

They made love again but didn't linger for long afterward. "Jump in the shower and come to the kitchen."

"You're not going to shower with me?"

"Maybe someday, but not here. Did you see my shower? It's no bigger than a phone booth." She laughed. "I've never been in one, but I've seen 'em in movies."

A short while later, he walked into the kitchen. All of the previous night's dishes were washed and put away, as were any leftovers. He wondered what time she had gotten up. A cup of steaming coffee was waiting at his place.

"I collected eggs yesterday. You want fried, scrambled, or an omelet?

"What's in the omelet?"

"Choosy beggar, are you?" she kidded. "Leftovers from last night."

"Okay, I'm game. I'll have a spaghetti omelet. It'll be a change from my usual scrambled at the restaurant."

"I don't have any bread for toast, but there's more mango bread."

"Just the omelet with some pepper will be fine."

Five minutes later, she served them each a mushroom, watercress, and goat-cheese omelet. They ate in silence and in a hurry. Her coffee must have cooled some, but he had to slurp his because it was so hot. He carried his plate to the small counter next to the sink. She took his cup and poured the rest into a paper Akamai carry-out cup and popped a lid on it.

"I'll assume that was one of your used ones and not company pilfering."

Lia grinned, lifted one eyebrow, and remained mute. She walked him out onto the lānai. He slid into his slippers, set the coffee cup on the railing, displacing a gecko that leapt out of the way, and hugged her as a prelude to a tender kiss. Their eyes locked onto each other's. He had held it in long enough and had to tell her.

"I love you, Lia." He saw the tiny smile come to her lips.

"I love *you*, Kekoa. Now go solve a murder!"

✦ ✦ ✦

CHAPTER 22

"**W**HAT ARE YOU doing?" asked Lia in response to Kekoa nuzzling her neck.

"Smelling you. I love the smell of your skin."

They were lying in bed together. They hadn't been together the night after the spaghetti dinner, because Kekoa had been called out on another stabbing death, unrelated to his case. Still, they both realized they wanted to spend more nights together. Kekoa hadn't moved in, but he did bring his clothes for work the next day.

"What are you doing next Saturday?" asked Lia.

"Not tomorrow but next week? No real plans. Why, you want to do something?"

"You know what a first-birthday lūʻau is?"

"Of course. Remember—I was born and raised here. Hmm, I wonder if my folks gave me one. I'll have to ask."

Lia gave him a playful poke in the ribs. "Enough about you." She rolled over, halfway onto him, and he enjoyed the feel of her breast squeezing against his chest. "My brother and his wife are having one for my new niece at their house. Would you go with me?"

"I'm going to meet the family *already*?" he teased. "Of course, I'll go," his tone serious this time.

"You'll get to see the house where I grew up, and, yes, meet my mom and brother, and sister-in-law and nephew and nieces. But, babe, I need to tell you something."

He had instantly noticed the introduction of the pet name but also the change in the tone of her voice.

"A former boyfriend of mine is likely to be there. We broke up over a year ago, but he just won't let it go."

"Sweetie, everyone past sixth grade has history, but I appreciate you telling me. His being there won't bother me.

"Was it serious?"

"We went together for two years, but when he asked me to marry him, I said no. I was still going to school then. So he was naturally hurt, but also angry, which is the main reason I said no. I'd seen his angry outbursts before, and they scared me. I wasn't about to marry a guy I have to worry about him hitting me someday."

"Smart girl. I don't blame you."

"My mom and brother understood, but he works with my brother, and I imagine all the guys not on duty at his station will at least have been invited."

"I'm not going to have to fight him, am I?"

"Stop. On the other hand, I might enjoy that," she laughed.

"It's getting late. I'd better get ready for work."

"Let's make love first. You can skip a shower this morning."

"Oh, go in smelling like sex?"

"Won't *they* be jealous," she teased.

When they were finished, she said, "Go shave and I'll make a quick breakfast. I have bread now. How about a fried-egg sandwich with mango jam?"

+ + +

CHAPTER 23

DETECTIVE ANASTASIA "Stays" Chang got off the phone and announced to the team, "That was the crime lab at HPD . . ." The usual moans, grumbles, and negative comments followed, because Maui PD didn't have a crime lab and had to rely on the bigger, and therefore "more important" department on Oʻahu. "The semen was run through CODIS without results."

Bobby Ferko said, "If he wasn't in the combined federal or state index, he's never been to prison, probably never arrested for a felony, and never served in the armed forces."

"At least not in the *American* armed forces. We can't assume he's not an immigrant and maybe served somewhere else."

"Isn't there a way now to identify people by matching their DNA to a relative's DNA?" asked Detective Crane.

"There is," answered Kekoa, "but first you need a likely relative."

"Oh, yeah," said Roger. "I didn't think of that."

"No, you've got the right idea." Kekoa looked to make sure Anastasia was listening. "We need to send our suspect's DNA profile to GEDmatch in San Diego. It's a free DNA site for genetic genealogy research. If one of his relatives, the closer in affinity the better—"

"'Affinity'?" interjected Bobby. "Be careful, Kekoa—you need to define new words or big words for Roger." It got the expected laugh and an expected "payback's coming" smirk from Roger to Bobby.

Kekoa continued, "Like parents and siblings, but aunts, uncles, and first cousins are pretty good, too."

"Hell, half of Maui is a cousin to someone else on the island," offered Roger.

"Yeah, but I said 'first cousins'—anyone having at least one grandparent in common. In any case, GEDmatch will let us know if they get a hit in their system."

"I got to thinking of something else," said Bobby. "You know, campers at Waiʻānapanapa have to register and get a permit. Their contact info must be in the park-system computers someplace, right?

"What's something everyone does on vacation?"

"Takes photos!" replied Stays.

"Exactly. If no one has a problem with it, I'm going to track down everyone who was camping there that night and contact them; I'll ask them to email us all the photos they have that are not of their family or just plain nature photos. Maybe we'll see a person in the background who seems out-of-place, acting creepy, or whatever.

"Everyone camping there that night knew of the killing by the following morning, so many may be inclined to help even though they're already back in BF, Nebraska, or wherever."

"Great idea, Bob," said Kekoa, which Stays and Roger echoed.

KEKOA CALLED LIA as he left the headquarters building on his way to his car.

"Should I stop and pick up something for dinner? L&L? Panda Express?"

"We're having Hawaiian Chicken, and it's already in the oven. Do you like poi?"

"Is that a trick question? You know I'm related to Hāloa, right?"

"Pardon me, Mr. Kanaka. Make me feel inferior," she teased.

"Well, you get some slack because you *are* a native Hawaiian." He chuckled.

"And don't you forget it."

"Are you here yet?"

"Thirty or less if there are no wrecks. I love you."

"I love you, too."

BILL GRIFFIN'S DAD had picked him up at the airport the previous night. He had just returned from four weeks of Japanese immersion, living with a native family in the Sumisa ward of Tokyo. Not only was he getting college credit in his Japanese-language class at Maui College, but his conversational skills, including picking up idioms and slang, had increased immensely.

Today his dad had dropped him off at the mall for work, but, before clocking in at his assistant-manager job at the store that made customized ballcaps, he decided to make a quick trip to the parking garage and see if his truck would start or whether he'd have to call AAA for a jump.

He crossed the roadway from the mall into the garage and waited for his eyes to adjust to the still-dark cavern. When they did, he looked at the corner where he was *positive* he left his old Datsun. The space was empty. *What the fuck!* He walked over to the actual spot, as if that would somehow confirm the truck was gone, but did it anyway, more out of shock than anything else.

He stood there looking around. No, no one had moved the truck to a different spot as a joke. His gaze also wandered past the stairwell where the old lady with the Target cart slept. He often gave her a buck or two without her even asking. She was gone, too. Not just her and the cart but the whole little hovel she had set up under the stairs.

Well, standing there wasn't going to make the truck reappear. He'd better open the shop and then call the police to report the theft before shopper traffic began.

✦ ✦ ✦

CHAPTER 24

KEKOA GENTLY LIFTED his arm off Lia. They had been asleep, spooning, and he had had one arm tucked under his pillow and the other draped over his surfer girl. He carefully slid out of the bed to the narrow space where he could stand. Before he started staying over, she had the bed pushed against the wall, but he told her he needed room to get out so he didn't have to crawl over her if she was sleeping, like now.

He stopped at the end of the bed and looked down at her. The ambient light from the clock radio and the night light she kept on in the bathroom were enough to illuminate everything he needed to see. Her beautiful face relaxed in sleep, her lips slightly parted, and the explosion of hair on her pillow, partly covering her neck and one shoulder. There was no blanket, unneeded at this time of the year, and the single sheet came up just to her waist. He stood there for several seconds realizing, and still not believing, how lucky he was.

He had woken up thinking about the case and knew he wouldn't get back to sleep if he didn't write down some of the thoughts. In the kitchen, he got a pencil from the junk drawer, took an outdated note off the refrigerator door, and sat at the little dinette table. On the back of the paper, he started a list.

1. Who is this guy?
2. Resident or tourist?
3. Where's he from?
4. How did he get here?
5. How is he getting around?

He was tapping the pencil eraser on his forehead, trying to think of anything else, when Lia came in. She stood beside him, running her fingers through his hair.

"I felt you get out of bed. Can't sleep, babe?"

"Nah. Too much on my mind."

He sensed her reading his note. "Any ideas?" he asked as he reached around and pulled her closer, appreciating the soft firmness of her bare bottom.

"Tourist," she said with emphasis.

"Why?"

"Don't know. Just feel it in my na'au."

"Sorry for waking you," he said, turning toward her and nuzzling her tawny, bikini-trimmed muff.

"Don't start. I'm tired. Come back to bed. It's late." She turned and padded back down the hall.

Kekoa sat there a while longer, trying to think of anything else he was missing or that the team hadn't thought of. Part of him resented his department inserting him into the middle of this investigation and everyone expecting him to work some kind of miracle just because he got lucky on one murder case and went to the NHIA school. He really liked Anastasia and had been reluctant to step on her leadership role. She was sharp, and he wasn't surprised she was top on the sergeant's list, but it seemed she was always deferring to him. So be it. Tomorrow he would start exercising a little command authority and see if there was any pushback.

"YOU'RE UP EARLY," mumbled Lia from her pillow.

"Made a decision last night. Have to be the first one in. Have I ever told you how beautiful you are?"

"You have, but don't worry; I'll never get tired of hearing it."

He leaned down, pushed the hair off her face, and kissed her cheek. "I love you."

"I'll never get tired of hearing that, either," she said, smiling.

AS THE REST of the homicide team arrived, they saw a whiteboard repositioned at the head of what had been designated "the conference table."

1. Who is this guy?
2. Resident or tourist?
3. Where's he from?
4. How did he get here?
5. How is he getting around?

Kekoa had already spoken to Anastasia to make sure she didn't mind his "chairing" this morning's meeting.

"Aloha kakahiaka, team. I've asked the lieutenant to join us, so we'll get started as soon as he arrives. In the meantime, look at this list. It's not exhaustive, so if you can think of anything we should add, speak up."

He noticed Ferko and Crane look over at Stays and saw her nodding back, letting them know she was cool with him handling the presentation.

Lt. Dayrit came in, looked around, read the list on the board, and pulled up a chair at the opposite end of the table.

"Good morning, Lieutenant. Thank you for coming.

"Part of this is a gripe session, and we're going to need you to carry the news upstairs.

"My first day, the chief told me to expect a little animosity about an 'outsider' being brought in on an MPD case. Well, I've never felt that from you or any of this team, and whatever *they* felt," he tilted his head back toward the Investigations room, "they got over in one day.

"Then this referring to the four of us as 'the Serial Murder Task Force.' In my experience, a task force is a multi-agency function and generally more than four investigators. The name doesn't bother us, but it's the sense, maybe wrongfully interpreted by all of us here, that the troops think we don't need their help.

"But Loo, we all pretty much agree, with the exception of Hāna Division, we're getting shunned by the other patrol divisions. Yes, even this one. You send our memos upstairs to the captain to forward on to the Patrol captains, asking them to provide some legwork, and all we get is shade."

"Give me an example," said the lieutenant, his tone not happy.

"Well, for instance, we asked Lāhaina Patrol to canvas the houses two blocks south and two blocks mauka of the first killing, asking for permission to view people's home-security footage, if they had an outside camera, including doorbell cameras.

"So far, nothing. Not even a report of negative results. Was the canvas done or not? I'll tell you, they're going to be pretty embarrassed if we have to go up there and do it ourselves and we come up with something.

"And you know how the press is on this. Not good if we find something that patrol missed, and they learn about it."

Stays spoke up, "Yeah, Loo. I heard the Maui reporter for *Civil Beat* is getting ready to rake the department over the coals in her Saturday article. She's generally very fair with us but not now, with her readership foaming at the mouth."

Kekoa looked at the lieutenant and nodded in agreement. The lieutenant nodded back, acknowledging the point had been made.

Kekoa continued. "I've heard of investigators bringing in psychics on cases—" He held up both palms out in front of his chest as soon as he saw eyebrows go up. "I'm not suggesting that here, but neither do I discount gut feelings. A native Hawaiian told me they believe it's a stranger, not a local.

"I know, I know, that doesn't mean anything, but it got me thinking. What if the guy *is* a tourist? He didn't swim here. If we can get any kind of camera shot from the night of the Lāhaina killing, we can go to the airport and start going through TSA footage, maybe find out where he came from and what his name is.

"Also, we can't assume what we call 'Murder Number One' was, in fact, his first killing. What if there were others preceding it? We can narrow that down, maybe eliminate it, by learning when he arrived.

"Anything else?" asked Dayrit.

"Yes, Number 5," he replied, pointing at the board.

"The killer might've hitchhiked to Hāna but doubtful he came back the same way. Odds are he's stolen a car or truck. We know the guys out there," nodding again to the Investigations room, "have their own cases to work, and Stays asked Detective Ashdown for this, but we sense it got moved to Number 2 on his 'to do' list.

"We need names and contact info for the owners of all vehicles stolen in Wailuku and Lāhaina Divisions since the date of the Lāhaina murder. They need to be contacted to find out if their vehicle has been returned or otherwise located, even if it was abandoned and burned. Oh, and thefts in the Kīhei area can be ignored for right now. We don't think he's gone that far south."

"Gut instinct again?"

"No, auto-theft experience."

"Anything else?"

Kekoa looked at Stays and saw that she agreed the lieutenant was getting impatient. Was he mad at them, or was there going to be some imminent ass-chewing elsewhere?

"Yes, one last thing, and I expect this will have to come from an assistant chief or maybe even the Chief.

"The almighty HPD Crime Lab treating us like bastard stepchildren is bullshit. Do they have a serial killer working on Oʻahu? Then how about a little inter-agency cooperation and move our work requests to the top of the list."

The lieutenant nodded in agreement. "You guys are doing good work. Keep it up. I've got to go push some shit back uphill."

After the door closed, the quartet looked at each other, breathed a sigh of relief, and smiled.

"Good presentation, Kekoa," said Anastasia, and the others all chimed in with their agreement.

Stays stood up. "We're at a bit of a standstill for the moment, so let's all go back over our notes and see if there's anything we missed. And when we've finished with that, we're going to exchange notes and double-check each other."

✦ ✦ ✦

CHAPTER 25

BOBBY AND ROGER went out to lunch, Anastasia went home to give her mother-in-law a break, and Kekoa raced down to Kīhei to meet Lia.

He pulled into the Times Market parking lot across from her shop and found her waiting at the barbeque stand near the driveway. She jumped into his car with three bags, two white and one from Akamai. He pulled out onto Lipoa and drove to the end of the block. He took the blanket from the backseat, and they walked a ways down the beach and spread the blanket on the grass above the high-tide zone where beach morning glories were creeping makai.

"What did you get us?"

"Pulled-pork sandwiches and beach-friendly bottles of iced tea—recyclable plastic."

"I see that. Mmm, this smells good."

"Extra barbeque sauce if you want it, and lots of napkins, so you don't look sloppy when you go back to work." She saw his smirk out of the corner of her eye.

"How was work, by the way? Did they agree with your list?"

"They did, and so did the lieutenant, who we think will get us some help from upstairs."

"Is that where the bosses are?"

"Yep. The 'brass,' as we call them.

"How's your day going?"

"The usual. Smiles from the hurry-in, hurry-out locals who work nearby, young teens hanging out on their phones, older customers reading a book or Kindle, and the usual self-important tourists. They're not all that way—some are nice, but there's plenty of the other kind. Like the ones who cop an attitude because we don't have the same menu as Starbucks. We smile and say 'Sorry,' when we want to scream, 'You want Starbucks, go to frickin' Starbucks!'"

Kekoa laughed out loud at her performance, nearly choking on his sandwich and needed a quick swallow of his tea. He crumbled up his sandwich wrapper and napkins and put them in the bag. He handed her his empty bottle. "Will you take this with you for recycling?"

"You're finished already?"

"I'm not leaving. Take your time. I just like being with you, but then I need to get back."

"Really? I thought we might have time for some afternoon delight."

Kekoa chuckled. "Oh, so I can go in smelling like sex *again*? I think your nickname should be 'Āpiki."

Lia lifted her chin, wanting a definition.

"Mischievous, naughty, rascal, among other unrelated meanings."

Lia laughed. "OK, that's me *sometimes* . . . but you love it," she added with a twinkle in her eye.

Kekoa pushed her down on the blanket. "You bet I do." They exchanged a few kisses, and then he said, "I have to go. But I'll take a rain check."

"Well, we'll see," she smirked.

When Lia got out of the car back at the parking lot, she said, "I thought kolohe was mischievous and naughty."

"You're that, too, sweets!" he said, chuckling. "See you tonight."

When he looked in his rearview mirror for one more glance at her, he saw she was sticking out her tongue at him. *Ha! Kolohe for sure!*

✦ ✦ ✦

CHAPTER 26

ONE CASE STARTED making progress that same afternoon. Unfortunately, it wasn't theirs.

"The crime lab in Honolulu called and said they had a make on the footprint from the highway murder," announced Roger. "The lab said the sole print was definitely made from a Hi-Tec brand hiker called the Ravus.

"If he doesn't change shoes, it might help with an ID," said Bobby Ferko.

"And if a thousand guys on Maui don't already wear that same make and model," opined Stays. "Still, it's progress."

"Actually, once a shoe is worn, it develops little nicks and cuts on the sole that allow an expert to make a positive comparison," Kekoa informed them.

"Yeah, great for Investigations, but it doesn't help us," said Anastasia. "Put the info in an email, Roger, and send it to whoever has the case next door."

A little later, Detective Yamada came in. "The lieutenant pulled me off my fraud cases to help Ashdown on your auto thefts, and I found something interesting."

"Yeah?" they seemed to all ask in unison.

"This vic had his pickup stolen from the parking garage at the mall where the second murder took place."

"That's great, Darryl!" said Anastasia. "Make us a copy of the report and we'll go see him today. Kekoa, you want to roll out with me?"

"Sure, Stays, let's go."

Kekoa was reading the crime report as Anastasia pulled her unmarked police car out of the parking lot. "The guy lives upcountry, but he works at the mall. Let's try there first."

The detectives found the victim, William Griffin, working at the cap store on the upper level of the mall. He was wearing a striped referee's shirt, in keeping with the store's huge inventory of caps for every team sport in America, from college to pro.

After they determined which employee he was, Stays introduced herself.

"Mr. Griffin, I'm Detective Chang," she pulled back the right side of her blazer to reveal the badge on her belt, "And this is my partner, Detective Opio.

"We read in the police report that you parked your truck in the garage but don't know when it was stolen. How's that?"

"I was in Japan for a month for a language-immersion class. I went to check on it the morning after I got back—my dad picked me up at the airport and we went straight home. We live in Makawao. Anyway, when I came to work the next morning, I went to see if the battery was still charged, and the truck was gone."

"The mall security didn't mind you parking your truck there for a month?"

"Well, obviously it wasn't there the whole month, was it?"

"We're just gathering facts, Mr. Griffin . . ."

"I had permission from the mall owners to park it there. Any mall employee can ask for the same privilege. It had an official placard with the permission on the driver's side dash."

"And you're sure it was locked."

"Even if it wasn't locked doesn't give someone permission to steal it!"

"Of course not, Mr. Griffin. About the locks . . ."

"Both cab doors were locked, like I told the first officer. I had it parked in a corner on the first level. The right side was so tight against the wall I was worried about scraping my mirror. The truck had a camper shell with a drop-down door in the back, the kind that closes on top of the tailgate."

The detectives nodded that they understood the type he was describing.

"The lock on the camper door was broken, so that was another reason I parked in the corner. I backed up until the bumper touched the wall. The door would only have been able to open several inches, and the same for the tailgate. It would have taken a contortionist to wiggle into the little space."

"Probably. It's more likely the thief jimmied the door lock. It's easier to do on those older models."

"You know Datsuns are no longer made, and the '78 is considered a classic," Griffin said in a tone that implied he didn't think they realized that. "The paint was faded, but the engine ran great. Changed the oil every 3,000 miles."

"Good to know," said Anastasia, like she was impressed with that information. "It wasn't in the report, but we need to double-check something, and I want you to know you won't be in trouble with us if the answer is 'yes,' so it's important you be truthful."

"OK," he said, a bit reluctant after hearing the intensity of her prelude.

"Did you have a firearm in the glove box or anywhere else in the truck?"

His eyes got big, and his volume increased. "Absolutely not! I don't even have one at home!"

"Thank you, good to know." Anastasia looked at Kekoa. "Do you have any questions, detective?"

"Two questions, Mr. Griffin. How much gas did you have in your truck?"

"What does that have to do with my truck being stolen?!" the man exclaimed.

"Mr. Griffin, I don't waste my time or yours asking useless questions. Those little trucks get pretty good mileage, right?" The man nodded. "For one, it tells me how far the thief may have been able to go before needing to buy gas."

"Oh, yeah," the man said sheepishly. "Okay, you know how you get condensation in your gas tank as the car cools down overnight?"

"Yes, sir, I do."

"The emptier the tank, the more water that gets in your gas. Well, even being parked in the shade all day, it still gets hot in that garage, so I made a point of filling it up before I left."

"Thank you. That makes sense."

"Okay, here are the final questions. You said you were parked on the bottom deck. Did you see a homeless woman camping under a stairwell at night?"

Griffin gave Kekoa quizzical look and guessed it didn't have to do with his truck.

"Sure. Old Tasha, the bag lady. She had been living there for months. She was harmless. Management tried to run her off a few times, but after she alerted Security of a few auto break-ins in progress, they just let her stay. She was seldom there during the day. Left with her cart in the morning and didn't come back until sundown."

"Did you ever speak with her?"

"Sure. After I realized she was going to be a fixture there, I'd wave or say 'Hi' whenever I saw her. My truck was parked at the same end of the garage as her stairwell, just in the opposite corner. As a matter of fact, I gave her twenty bucks before I left for Japan and asked her to keep an eye on my truck. Then I came back and the truck was gone—and so was she."

"I'm sorry to inform you that she is dead. Someone murdered her."

"Oh, my God! You don't think she got killed trying to stop someone from taking my truck, do you?"

"Highly unlikely. I wouldn't give it another thought."

The detectives exchanged a look and nodded, and Anastasia thanked him for his time. She gave him her business card and said to call if he thought of anything else.

When the two got to the car, Anastasia said, "You can drive," and tossed him the keys. He had to slide the seat back. On the short drive up the hill to headquarters, she got on the radio to Dispatch.

"This is Detective Chang. Please broadcast an all-points bulletin to stop a faded-green, 1979 Datsun pickup truck with a white camper shell, and detain the driver." She read the license plate number off the crime report. "The driver should be considered armed and dangerous. I am to be notified personally, day or night, if the vehicle is stopped."

"Copy, detective. It just went out to all stations and MDCs."

+ + +

CHAPTER 27

"THAT WAS GOOD, Babe. No, I take that back. It was great."

"Yes, you were," said Kekoa, smiling down on his tan surfer girl.

They were both covered with sweat, and the day hadn't even heated up yet.

"This is the way every Saturday should begin," he said.

"Unless the surf is up." She gave him a nudge. "Time to get off . . ."

"I thought I just did."

She gave a spank on his ass and shoved. "You're getting too heavy."

Kekoa rolled off and stayed alongside her long, sleek body, sliding his index finger through the perspiration on her stomach, stopping to make a circle around her navel, then slowly running up the groove in the center of her ab muscles to the valley between her breasts.

"Are you staying over tonight?"

"Probably not," he replied as his finger circled her right nipple. "My aunt expects me to go to church with them in the morning."

"Isn't that kind of hypocritical? Make love to me and then go to church? And stop that—you're turning me on."

He was watching her nipple harden. "I suppose so. Isn't that what church is for? A hospital for sinners?"

"Do you think we're sinners?"

"You're Catholic. What do you think?"

She shrugged. After a few moments she said, "I know I love you and enjoy making love with you."

The perspiration had evaporated as his finger moved over dry skin to the other nipple.

"Does that tickle? You're not wet anymore?"

She had felt him stiffening against her thigh and reached down for him. "Oh, yes, I am. Okay, one more time. Let's go real slow this time."

"HI, LIA," SAID Miki'ala after seeing the name on the screen.

"Hi, Miki. Listen, I'm cramping really bad, so I'm not going to go tonight."

"You know what Kumu is going to say."

"I don't care. I took a Midol plus an 800-milligram ibuprofen, and I'm still curled up on the couch."

"I guess that means I won't go either unless I can find someone to come down here and get me. My truck is still in the shop."

"That's what you get for letting your boyfriend work on it. Why can't he drive you?"

"He's working his other job at the restaurant."

"Well, if you can get over here somehow, you can use my truck. I just filled it up. Come if you can, but I'm going to hang up now."

ONE THING ABOUT Maui, once the sun went down, it got dark in a hurry. Miki'ala was driving home from hula practice on a dark stretch of road through a wooded area when a truck behind her flashed his lights. *Why doesn't he just pass? The road is wide open.* The truck came alongside, trying to signal her to roll down her window. Once they had lowered their windows, he shouted that the surfboard was loose and might fall off.

She pulled over, and he pulled over behind her, offering to help. She climbed up on the rear bumper and checked. The board was strapped down tight. She had barely jumped down and turned to tell him when his hands grabbed her throat and started choking.

✦ ✦ ✦

CHAPTER 28

As a MEMBER, albeit a temporary one, of the Maui Police Department, Kekoa had the use of the workout room at police headquarters and took advantage of it after work on Tuesdays and Thursdays, when Lia had hula practice. When he came out of the men's locker room, he could hear the clang of metal plates hitting each other and the sound of someone pummeling the heavy bag. As he got closer, he recognized the attacker as Anastasia. Her usual blazer, blouse, and slacks had been replaced with shorts, sport bra, and a tank top. She had also replaced her usual French braid with a ponytail that was whipping back and forth as she did high kicks to the bag.

When she stopped to catch her breath, Kekoa said, "That was impressive, Stays."

She grinned and nodded an acknowledgment of the compliment.

"I don't remember seeing you in here on a Thursday," he said.

"Yeah, I'm usually Monday, Wednesday, and Friday, but I missed yesterday. Good for my husband to spend time with kiddo. He doesn't mind me staying late to work out, anyway. He's almost as interested as I am in getting back in shape. Love the baby, but they wreak havoc on your body." She wiped her face with her towel. "Well, a two-mile sprint on the treadmill and I can go home . . . if my breasts don't explode first."

The whole team knew she was breast feeding and took time during the day to express the milk stored in "Do Not Drink"-labeled containers in the unit's refrigerator.

Kekoa did his usual twenty minutes on the elliptical machine programmed for varying speeds and elevations before hitting the weights. He was doing dead lifts when he saw the message light on his phone flashing on the bench next to him. When he finished the set, he looked at the message and saw it was an alert sent out as a broadcast text from the lieutenant. "Older model Dodge Laramie, side of the road, wooded area of Pukalani. Engine running, lights on, no driver. Might be our killer again. One of you should respond. Call for backup if needed."

He looked up and saw Anastasia coming out of the locker room. She had already showered and dressed. When their eyes met, she held up her phone, and he did likewise, acknowledging the message.

"Take my car," she said. "Keys are in the top drawer. I have to run home first and will come back for another car."

"No, take your car and come as soon as you can. I'll grab a cruiser."

He ran into the locker room, stripped off his gym clothes and pulled on his pants, shoes, and shirt. The whole time his guts were in a knot. Lia's hālau was in Pukalani, and she drove a Laramie.

He ran down the hall, getting looks from two uniformed officers walking by, and burst into their conference room. He had already pulled out his key ring and immediately unlocked his desk, pulled open the top left drawer and took out his gear. He took his pistol from the holster and laid it on the desk. His other hand had been unbuckling his belt, the dress version of the Bullhide gun belt. He pulled out the left side of the belt, slid his double magazine pouch on, did another pants loop with the belt and slipped on his cuff case, another pants loop, and ran the belt through the back slot on the holster, another belt loop, and the forward holster slot. After buckling the belt, he clipped his badge just forward of it. He did a press check on his pistol to ensure it was hot and holstered the weapon.

When he got into the hall, he hesitated for a moment, getting his bearings. Where was Patrol located? Remembering, he turned left and hustled down the hall.

Thank God, the Patrol lieutenant is at his desk!

"Loo, I'm Detective Opio from Investigations . . ."

"Yeah, the murder cop from San Diego," he said cheerfully. "How's that going?"

"We think something is breaking tonight, right *now*! Do you have a marked unit I can borrow?"

The lieutenant picked up on the stress in the detective's voice. He got up and took two quick, giant steps to a peg board, removed a key ring, and tossed if to Kekoa. "Number 257. Fill it up when you come back."

"One other thing, do you have a four-cell I can borrow?"

"No, sorry, but here, take this," and tossed him the six-inch Streamlight from his own gunbelt. "Just make sure I get it back!"

"Absolutely. Thanks, Loo," shouted Kekoa as he ran toward the back lot.

He didn't want to switch to emergency equipment too close to the station, but it took him more than a block once he was out of the police lot before he found the correct switch, anyway, when he activated the overhead lights and siren. He didn't know what MPD's policy was for using them, but he wasn't in a pursuit, which was the usual heartburn for department brass, and, besides, what were they going to do, fire him?

One thing about Maui he was thankful for, drivers were quick to pull to the curb when emergency vehicles had to get past. Thus, he made a super smooth run down Ka'ahumanu Avenue, took the turn onto Hāna Highway a little too fast, skirted the east side of Kahului and headed up Haleakalā Highway.

He wanted more information, but tying up radio traffic to ease his curiosity wasn't going to get him there any faster and only make him more worried if the wrong reply came back. He turned off the siren when he reached Pukalani and radioed Dispatch for directions to the scene. He thought he might vomit as his unit's lights illuminated the silver-gray pickup with the surf rack and personalized stickers on the other side of the road, where there were two marked units, blinking blue-and-white emergency lights on. He left his emergency equipment on as well and parked directly across the road from Lia's truck. He knew it was selfish and irrational to think it at this time, but he couldn't help himself: *What am I going to do if anything has happened to her?*

The officer who had first found the abandoned truck was parked slightly in echelon behind it, his unit's driver-side tires slightly on the roadway and its blue-and-white lights still blinking. The young officer had laid out road flares farther behind his unit and was directing traffic to slow down with his flashlight. Kekoa nodded to him as he jogged across the road and over to the patrol sergeant, who was monitoring traffic coming the other direction.

"Detective Opio, Sarge. Can you fill me in on what you know so far?"

"Not much. Officer Smith," he left it to be implied the young guy was Smith, "rolled up on the truck pulled over on the shoulder. The driver's door was standing open, the lights were on, and the engine was running. He thought maybe the driver stopped to puke or pee, but no one was around."

"Has the area been searched?"

"I don't believe so."

"Are more units rolling?"

"I requested help as soon as I got here—must be fifteen or twenty minutes now. Dispatch promised help as soon as units cleared from other calls."

"Thanks, Sarge. I'll go talk to Smith and see if he has anything he forgot to tell you."

Kekoa walked down the shoulder, almost nauseous as he got to Lia's truck. He looked inside but didn't see anything out of the ordinary; he didn't see her purse. He reached the young patrolman. Luckily, no cars were coming right then.

"Officer, I'm Detective Opio . . ."

"Oh, yeah, from the homicide task force," he said, impressed. Kekoa forced himself not to roll his eyes. "You're that murder cop they brought in from San Diego."

"Word travels fast." He kept talking as the officer signaled an oncoming vehicle. "One quick question, Officer. After you arrived, did you search the area at all?"

"Not really. I ran my light on the ground around the truck looking for blood or any personal items and then scanned into the woods calling out that the police were here, but I didn't see or hear anything."

"Thanks, Officer. You did good."

Kekoa walked back to his marked cruiser, got in, and phoned his lieutenant.

"I've been waiting to hear something," was the greeting. "Whatcha got?"

"It doesn't look good. Abandoned truck, with engine and the lights on, driver's door standing open. No one around.

"Only two units here and they're directing traffic. The sergeant said he's asked for more units, but none so far. I need you to light a fire under someone's ass and get some help up here. But not that Lt. McAvenia. He's a straight shooter, and I don't think the request made it to him.

"Also, does the department have any tracking dogs?"

"Of course. All our canines are cross-trained, patrol and one other specialty."

"We could use at least one tracker up here PDQ. Stays is en route; I'll call the rest of the team."

"No, they'll come quicker if I call them. Call back if you need anything else or want me to come up."

"Thanks, Loo."

ANASTASIA SAID THEY would debrief and write their reports in the morning. Kekoa had returned the cruiser, filled it with gas, and returned the lieutenant's flashlight. He signed a form to have Lia's truck released to him. He got approval from the lieutenant to have an officer drive his car home and another officer to follow them and ferry the first officer back to the station.

Kekoa pulled into the driveway past Lia's cottage and then backed into her parking space between the rock wall and the cottage. He walked out to the street, showed the officer where to park his car, and thanked them both for the courtesy.

He slowly climbed the steps to the lānai, tired, but so happy to be home. *Home—is that what I consider it now?* He could tell one of the end-table lamps was on but not if Lia was still up. He rapped lightly on the door and waited. No response. He tried one more time a little harder, and he could feel the vibration of her bare feet on the floor even out there on the lānai. He heard the deadbolt turning, and there she was.

"Hi, Babe. Why didn't you use your key? That's what it's for," she teased.

He just looked at her, not sure if he'd ever seen anything so beautiful. He took her into his arms and hugged her, a full body-to-body embrace, as he kissed her intensely.

"Do you know how much I love you?"

"A lot, it seems."

"I don't think I really realized how much I love you until I thought I had lost you."

"Why would you ever think that?"

"I thought you might've been a victim of the serial killer."

"What?!"

"But it was Miki'ala he stopped . . . "

She pushed herself away from him to see his face more clearly. "No! Is she, is she okay?"

"Yes, she's fine. A little shaken up, but she kept her wits about her and got away. Mosquito bites and minor scratches from running into a dark woods is all.

"Oh, Lia. I love you so much."

"I love you, too, honey," said, starting to realize he was as traumatized as Miki must be.

"I want to, *need* to be with you."

She gave him a crooked grin. "I'm think I'm getting my period."

"I know. Miki'ala told me. Does that bother you?"

"No. Does it bother you?"

"No."

"Get undressed. Let me go wash up."

✦ ✦ ✦

CHAPTER 29

BASED ON WHAT he had said at the door, Lia thought she would be ravished as soon as she got in bed, but, instead, he just wanted to hold her.

"Lia, I can't explain how I felt when I got up there and saw your truck. The call had said it was found abandoned with the engine running, the headlights on, and the driver's door standing open."

He was quiet for a while just hugging her and stroking her hair. It was making her hot, but she didn't want to interrupt him. She could wait to turn on the air conditioner. Then he resumed.

"A tracking dog arrived, and she and her handler went into the woods. The dog had picked up somebody's scent. The rest of us were all fanned out on either side with flashlights.

"Real soon, he yelled, 'Found her!' I'm sorry, sweetheart. I don't know why I was prepared for the worst . . ."

Lia could tell he was on the verge of tears. "It's okay, baby, I'm here; I'm okay."

"I went crashing through brush and branches to where the canine officer was. A lot of flashlights were converging. I didn't want to look, but I did, and it wasn't you." He sniffled. "It was Miki'ala! I noticed right away she still had her shorts on, and someone said, 'She's alive.'

"Don't know who, maybe the patrol sergeant, but someone had already requested EMTs, and they came in with their box, checked her vitals and stuff. They said she was just unconscious. We would see the big, red bump on her forehead, and half a dozen flashlights went up at the same time to a branch right above her with skin and blood on it. I was kneeling next to her, calling her name without success. One of the medics cracked a smelling-salt vial under her nose, and she came to.

"As soon as she saw me, she sat up and hugged me. I asked her where you were and she said, 'At home. I borrowed her truck.' I felt like a balloon losing its air. They took Miki to the hospital to spend the night for observation and to treat all the kiawe wounds and mosquito bites."

It was then she first noticed the scratches and bites on his arms and face. "Tell me the rest in the morning . . . and we're *going* to sleep in. Do you still want to make love? If not . . . "

"Yes, I do. And I see you already put down the purple towel."

Lia snickered. "Just in case. Let me jump up and turn on the A/C real quick."

MIKI'ALA WAS SITTING on the edge of the bed, draped in one of those stiff paper hospital gowns. It didn't smell like calamine lotion, but her legs, arms, and neck were dappled with some kind of flesh-colored ointment. A gauze strip was holding a larger gauze dressing to her forehead.

"I'm telling you, I'm fine. I've been bitten by mosquitoes and stabbed with kiawe thorns my whole life and it never killed me. Just give me something for this godawful headache and I'll be outta here," Miki'ala complained to the nurses.

"That concussion could kill you, and you're staying here for the night. You'll be taken for an MRI shortly. Once a doctor reviews the slides, we'll have a better idea what's going on. You wouldn't want to go home with bleeding on the brain and not know about it, would you?"

Miki'ala didn't answer and looked over to the door, where a plainclothes female police officer had just come in. She was wearing a blouse and slacks, and had a gun and badge on her belt on one side and something else in a leather case on the other hip.

Anastasia addressed the older of the two nurses. "Good evening. I'm Detective Chang. If it's okay, I'd like to get a quick interview with Miss Kanae."

"That's fine," the nurse said, "until the orderlies come to take her for the MRI."

"Okay, great. I'll be quick."

"Hello, Ms. Kanae. I'm Detective Chang. Can you tell me what you remember about the incident upcountry?"

"Not really. There were so many people. Everything's kind of a blur until I got here."

Anastasia turned on her pocket recorder and set it on the table over the bed. "I remember seeing Kekoa when I came to, and paramedics . . . and was there a dog there?"

"Yes, there was. That was Māla. She found you.

"What about earlier, before you ran in the woods? Do you remember that?"

"Oh, yeah. I remember that just fine."

"Tell me what you remember."

"I was coming home from hula practice. I was driving my friend Lia's truck. This little truck came up behind me and kept flashing his lights. I thought, *What the hell, there's plenty of room—just go ahead and pass me.* Eventually, he pulled up alongside me and was motioning for me to pull over. *Sure, buddy, that's just what I'm going to do on a dark road.* But then I saw him reaching across the seat and rolling down the window. How old *was* that truck? I thought all cars and trucks had power windows these days. So, I put down the window and he yells, 'Your board is loose; it's going to slide off.' Well, that was all I needed—borrow Lia's truck and lose her good board. So, I pulled over and he pulled over behind me.

"Could you please reach that water for me?"

"Of course."

After taking a long drink, Miki'ala continued. "As I was getting out, I saw the guy was getting out of his truck, too, and said, 'Can I help?' I didn't want to be rude, but I wanted to be careful, so I left my door open in case I needed to jump in in a hurry. I walked around to the back and was about to climb up on the bumper to see about the board and thought, *If you wanted to help, why did you turn your headlights off?* The board looked fine; I tried shaking it and it was belted on tight. I stepped down off the bumper and was going to tell him he was mistaken, but, before I could say a word, he grabbed me by the throat and started choking me and moving me around to the passenger side of the truck. I thought I must be having a nightmare or something—except my neck hurt and I was having trouble breathing. I had my hands on his wrists trying to pull him off when I remembered something I learned at a women's defensive class at the YMCA. I let go of his wrists, came over the top of his arms, and dug my thumbs into his eyes. I was nearly out of breath. He screamed and leaned back but didn't let go—his arms were longer than mine—so I grabbed his wrists again and pulled him toward me and kneed him in the nuts with everything I had. He bellowed like a stuck pig, and I just took off and ran into the woods."

"Impressive! Great narrative, Ms. Kanae, and congratulations on keeping your head and defending yourself like you did. That defensive-tactics class was worth every penny you paid for it.

"I think I have just one question. At any time, did he try to push your shorts down, or put one or both hands in your shorts, or grope your breasts, or rub up against you with an erection, or anything of a sexual nature?"

"No. I would have noticed something like that and not forgotten it."

"Thank you. One of my detectives will contact you in a few days to look at some photos, okay? It looks like they're ready to take you for that MRI. I think I have everything I need, but here's my card. Sometimes memories come back a day or two later. Please call me if you think of anything else."

✦ ✦ ✦

CHAPTER 30

THE TEAM ALL drifted in late the following morning and, over cups of coffee, slowly started working on their reports of the previous night. Like most modern departments, each detective wrote a report of why, what, when, and where about their individual involvement in the incident and a synopsis of any interviews. When Stays was finished with hers, which was probably the longest, as she had the victim statement to include in her report, she called the team to the conference table.

"I asked last night's victim if the perp ever tried anything sexual with her, and she was adamant he had not. I've interviewed rape victims before, and, if they haven't been drugged, most will say they screamed for help, at least until the guy hit them or threatened to kill them, or both. Even if our other victims screamed, how long did they do it, and who was nearby to hear it? A hooker in a dark alley, an old woman in a deserted parking garage, a young woman asleep in a tent.

"Last night's victim didn't say anything about screaming because she was fighting for her life. I got to thinking. We've been working under the impression that the victims were killed *after* being raped. What if this guy is doing them *after* he kills them?"

The three men were silent for several moments, digesting this new possibility, until Bobby said, "Necrophilia! That's fucking sick."

"Maybe the killing is what excites him sexually, and that's when he rapes the bodies," suggested Kekoa. "And even he knows how sick it is, and that's why he covers their faces so they can't 'look' at him." He saw Stays nodding, considering it.

"Hell, that's FBI Behavioral Science Unit shit. Way outside my pay grade," opined Roger. "I just want to catch a killer."

Around 10:00 a.m., Anastasia returned from briefing the lieutenant. After only a few minutes at her desk, she hurried back out. When she returned minutes later, she loudly proclaimed, "God bless officers who are willing to go the extra mile!

"Look what I just got from Lāhainā station." She held up three color pictures she had printed on the Investigations Division color printer. She walked over to the clean whiteboard and taped them up.

"A patrol officer was canvassing door to door . . ."

"I'll bet he wasn't the only one. Thanks, Lieutenant!" interjected Detective Crane.

"And he got these two profile shots from a house camera of a guy walking southbound on Waineʻe the night of the murder. There's a McDonald's behind him up on Waineʻe and Papalaua, so he takes a chance to see if their cameras got anything.

"Look at this! Compare the baseball cap, jacket, and shirt collar in the three photos. Same guy, but in this one, he's looking right into the damn camera. Smile, sucker!"

"That's more like an 'Oh, shit!' than a smile. And check the time stamp—2302. Right inside the ME's parameters for time of death," said Roger.

"This could be our guy," opined Bobby.

"Wait—it gets better. Let me see if the other photo got here." Anastasia went back to her desk and pulled up an email on her laptop. "It's here. I'm sending it over to the color printer; be right back."

She was back in less than a minute and taped up another photo.

"We were wondering how he got around. "The patrol officer knew there was a bus stop on Dickenson, just off Waineʻe, so he contacted the bus company and asked for the security tape from the bus that stopped there after 11:02 on our date. Who do you see paying his fare?" she asked rhetorically as she tapped the whiteboard.

"Who is this wonder cop?" asked Bobby.

"Manu Crozier."

"Any relation to Captain Crozier?"

"Nephew," answered Stays.

"The chief needs to send a nice commendation to that officer's command," said Kekoa. The idea received unanimous endorsement.

"I'll tell you something else," said Detective Crane, returning to the earlier topic. "My wife used to ride the bus to work for years. That's the Lāhainā Islander route, and where do you think its terminus is?"

"Terminus? Roger, you give me a woody when you use big words like that."

"Fuck you, Bobby."

The rest of the team all chuckled.

"The route *ends*, Bobby, my illiterate friend, at Queen Ka'ahumanu Mall!"

Stays looked at her three detectives. "Location of the Datsun and the bag lady. It's only circumstantial, but I think we've had another breakthrough."

"I'm going to run this news to the LT. If he gives the green light, we'll have one profile and the McDonald's photo sent to all the MDCs," she said, referring to the mobile dispatch computers in all the squad cars.

"I'll forward the photos to your laptops and print out three more for the murder books.

"Bobby and Kekoa, you go out to the airport and hook up with TSA or, more likely, the airport security. Start on the day of the first killing and work backwards as far as you can get, say, within four hours of all the arriving passengers. Roger and I will take a turn at it tomorrow."

Bobby looked at Kekoa but said it so everyone got the news. "I know exactly what camera we need to watch. The one that covers those two escalators and the stairs coming down from the concourse to baggage claim." The other two detectives nodded. They knew exactly the exit to which he was referring.

+ + +

CHAPTER 31

THAT BITCH, I should have killed her quicker, thought Del Kurtz. His balls still hurt, and his vision was still cloudy in one eye. She must have scratched the eyeball. He was going to watch for that truck, force her over, and pull her out of it by her hair, he decided. She might get rid of the MAUI HUB sticker on her tailgate, wherever or whatever the hell that was, or the faded mayor campaign sticker on her bumper, but she wouldn't lose the personalized SRFRGRL license plate. Worse, she had seen him. Stared right into his face and could probably identify the truck, too.

Nothing he could do about that now. Maybe she would be too scared or embarrassed to go to the police, but he couldn't count on that.

Right now, he was putting distance between him and that truck. Once that bitch disappeared into the woods, he took off. It was no use trying to catch her in the dark without a flashlight.

He was hungry, too. A lot of restaurants that had started curbside delivery during the COVID scare had maintained the practice, so he tried to find those places on his smartphone. It was a blessing the truck's previous owner had left his phone charging cord.

His only expenses were food and gas, and the cash from the tent girl had him flush right now, but without any income, he still had to be thrifty with what he had.

"INVESTIGATIONS. DETECTIVE CHANG."

Kekoa tried disguising his voice with high-pitched, feminine tone. "Investigations? Oh, I'm sorry. I was trying to reach the Homicide Task Force."

"Nice try, Opio. Whadaya want? I'm busy."

"I'm in the car on speaker with Bobby. Well, for number one, you can forget about coming to the airport and viewing hours of videos tomorrow."

"And that's because—"

"Because Bobby and I already found him. He came in the day of the first murder."

"That's good to know. Is there a number two?"

"There is. For number two, we have a name and a city of origin. His name is Delbert Kurtz, and he flew on a Saver Fare with Alaska Airline from Seattle. Took off at 0815 and got to Maui at 1130. Bobby ran him; he has no wants or warrants in Washington State. We'll check NCIC when we get back."

"Good work, guys. How did he get away from the airport?"

"Odds are he walked, hitchhiked, or begged a ride, but somehow he got to Lāhaina. Do you think that's worth pursuing?"

"Okay, leave it. Write it all up when you get back. Make sure hard copies get in the murder books. Oh, and call Roger with the perp's vitals so he can pull up his Washington driver's license photo and prepare a photo array."

After he disconnected, Kekoa turned to Bobby Ferko. "She sounds more like a sergeant every day," he kidded.

"Just missing the stripes, and she'll have those soon enough."

✦ ✦ ✦

CHAPTER 32

KEKOA HAD TO COME in the door sideways with all his paper shopping bags.

"What's all this?" inquired Lia as he set the parcels down on the little dinette table.

"Can't show up at a baby lūʻau without bringing food, so this is ours. You said you already had a present, so I'm doing my share. I have to go back out for the watermelon."

"Okay," Lia said quizzically, "but what is it going to be?"

"Fresh fruit bowls. Always a hit."

"And those are the bowls?" she asked, nodding to large, clear plastic bowls nested together in a Walmart shopping bag.

"Yeah, wanna help? You could wash the bowls. Do you have a colander?"

"Yes, I can, and yes, I do. How about take off your cover shirt—" she said, referring to the muted aloha shirt he wore over his gun when he wasn't on the clock. "And your gun; then come give me a kiss, and tell me about your day. I can tell you're amped."

"Not even three weeks, and you already know me that well?

"Okay. Let me change clothes." He went out onto the lānai and brought in his leather loafers and put them in the bedroom closet, returning shortly thereafter in just a pair of shorts. He gave Lia a big hug, and they kissed. She ran her hands down his muscular back and shoved them inside the elastic band of the shorts. "Oh, going commando, I see."

"Don't I most of the time when we're here?"

"Yes, but I thought we might walk down to the beach," she said and held up a bottle of wine.

"If we go down there and split a bottle of wine, you'll bring me back here and take advantage of me, and I'll never get the fruit bowls done."

"*Not even three weeks and you already know me that well?*" she mimicked, and they both laughed.

"How about we take the half bottle left from yesterday's dinner? We'll go to the beach, I'll tell you about major developments in the case, we'll come back here, knock out this salad, and eat dinner. We can't stay for the sunset tonight, though."

"I love a man with a plan as long as it ends with him taking me to bed."

Kekoa laughed. "You're so easy."

Lia snickered. "And you love it!"

THEY WERE WALKING back from the beach, Kekoa with the blanket and Lia with the backpack containing the empty bottle, and she said, "Those are giant steps forward in your case, sweetheart." He always noticed when she called him pet names besides "Babe" and liked them all. "When will you catch him?"

"Good question. The chief is taking major heat on this, and he'll hold a press conference tomorrow so everyone will have this guy's photo. There's been an APB out with the troops for two days on that truck and still no sightings. There can't be that many faded-green Datsuns!"

When they got to the house, Lia handed him the backpack. "Here, take in the stuff. I'll be right back. I want to talk to the neighbors."

"You mean your landlord?"

"Same thing," she said and stuck out her tongue at him.

When she got back, she asked, "How would you like to barbeque a steak for dinner?"

"Sure. After we do this fruit?"

"The fruit's not going to spoil that fast. No, now, silly. The neighbors are just finishing with their grill and said we could use it."

She took out a package from the refrigerator containing two ribeye steaks and four ears of corn. "I was planning on this for Sunday dinner, but we'll have it tonight. I won't have time to marinade the steaks, but what the heck."

"Here's the colander," she announced, removing it from one of the cabinets alongside the sink. "Will you pull off enough leaves from the lettuce to make our salads and rinse them in the sink and also that tomato on the counter? I'll be right back."

"Where did you go?" he asked when she got back a short while later.

"I put the corn on the grill."

"Oh. Smart."

"'Ae, akamai *nui* kāu hoa wahine."

He gave her a squeeze on the butt, smiling. "Yes, you are."

Lia gathered and twisted her long hair, tied it up on top of her head, and then removed the steaks from the package, salted and peppered them, and put them on a platter. "Babe, will you clear off the table, maybe put all the groceries in the corner for now? I'll get these started on the grill. Meet me there—just follow the smell."

Kekoa did follow the delicious odor of the cooking meat and carried two wineglasses of purple liquid without spilling a drop. Lia had her wineglass in one hand and the barbeque fork in the other, and was trying to push an errant strand of hair off her face with her wrist. Kekoa reached over and pushed it behind her ear.

"I remember the first time I did that," he said, smiling.

"So do I, and the luscious kiss that followed. And then you just left—and, from what you said at the bottom of the steps, I knew I was falling in love with you."

Kekoa smiled, happy to learn that. "You had me since, 'This is my beach.'"

Lia laughed. "Well, whatever it takes. We both won."

Kekoa smiled in acknowledgment. A man was approaching from the big house and Kekoa's radar turned on. He was a handsome man, maybe mid-50s, with a thick head of gray hair.

"Grill working okay, Lia?"

"Yes, thank you for letting us use it, Kevin."

"Sweetheart, this is my landlord, Kevin Richards."

"Nice to meet you. I'm Justin Opio." Their hands met in a manly handshake.

"So, you're a cop." The sentence was declarative, not interrogative.

Kekoa looked at Lia, and, instantly, their eyes exchanged a message like only lovers can do. "I didn't say a word," they told him.

Before Kekoa could respond to the man, he added, "I saw you coming in the gate a couple of times wearing your gun and badge."

"I'm a deputy sheriff, actually, just assigned here on a temporary assignment."

"How's Meredith doing in college?" asked Lia, to change the subject as she checked the corn husks.

"Quite well, actually. We thought she might have some trouble adjusting to college plus living away from home for the first time, but she's fine," Kevin said.

"Studying Oceanography at UC San Diego," Lia told Kekoa.

"Oh, neat. We can't live without the ocean," said Kekoa. Kevin smiled and lost it just as fast when Kekoa added, "E mālama i ke kai, right?"

"Well, I better get back to our company. Don't bother trying to clean the grill. I have some magic stuff you spray on, and all the grease and stuff just falls off."

"Thanks again for letting us use it," Lia said to the man's back as he headed toward the big house.

When they walked back to the cottage with the two platters and two glasses, Kekoa asked, "What was *that*? He doesn't like cops or doesn't like Hawaiians?"

"Ha! You picked up on that?"

"Of course. Deciphering tone and body language can keep a cop alive."

"Is that why you didn't tell him you lived in San Diego and your sister went to UCSD?"

"No, that was just not wanting to give out personal information that's none of his business."

"Listen," she said after they were back in their house, "They're nice to me, so I'm nice in return. Plus, they haven't raised my rent since I moved in. But he's a total haole," she said, her tone conveying it as the commonly used pejorative for snooty whites and not the literal meaning of anything foreign. "Thinks all kanakas are uneducated alcoholics, drug addicts, and living on welfare. Goes off on anything that smacks of the sovereignty movement, and that includes the hae Hawai'i and 'ōlelo Hawai'i."

They put it out of their minds and sat down to their salads, steaks, liberally buttered corn, and wine.

"Hey, what's this?" asked Lia, pointing her fork at the spray of pink-orange plumeria in her bud vase on the table.

"I saw your dusty little vase in the cupboard a few days ago and figured it was time I brought my lady some flowers."

Her eyes communicated everything she might have said as she leaned over and tenderly kissed him.

+ + +

CHAPTER 33

"Let me do the pineapple," Lia said. "I've had more practice than you."

"I'm sure you have, but fruit salad is my potluck specialty, so dice up the pineapple and cantaloupe kind of small, and put it in the bottom of both bowls. It works better if the firmer fruit is on the bottom, grapes and banana chunks in the middle, and the softer stuff, like the watermelon and mango, on top, or people stabbing around with the serving spoon turn it all to mush."

"Aye aye, sir."

They had washed and dried the dinner dishes and the party bowls so as to have a clean working area. Kekoa was plucking the green and purple seedless purple grapes from their stems and tossing them in the colander prior to washing. Half of the watermelon had been cubed and put in a mixing bowl for the time being.

"When you peel the mangoes, put the rinds in a soup bowl, please," requested Lia.

"Mango rind soup?"

"No, the chickens love them. Same with any grapes that aren't fit for the party."

When they were finished, they stopped to admire the layered colors of their contribution.

"We make a heck of a team, Lia," Kekoa said, putting an arm around her shoulder and pulling her closer.

"Don't you forget it, fella.

"I'm going to cover these with GladWrap and put them in the outside refrigerator on the neighbors' lānai. They've invited me to use it whenever I need to."

"Here, let me carry one."

When they came back to the cottage, Lia said, "I'm going to shower and get ready for bed. Do you want to try surfing in the morning? Yeah? Good. Turn on the TV, and let's try to catch the weather."

Lia came out wearing a towel and blotting her hair with another one. "Anything?"

"No weather or surf reports yet," Kekoa responded from his seat on the side of the bed.

"That's okay. I have four surf-report apps on my phone. I can check in the morning. You want to try north shore if it's up?"

Kekoa pulled off her towel, grabbed her buttocks, and pulled her mons into his face.

"What are you . . . Ohh, don't stop," she moaned as she held his head in her hands.

A while later, Lia breathed, "Thank you, Babe. You do that just right. I thought my legs were going to collapse."

Kekoa seductively licked his lips. "Sure glad I'm not a vegetarian," he sniggered.

"Hurry and take your shower and you can give me an encore."

THERE WERE NO waves the next morning, so Lia called a friend who brought over her stand-up board for Kekoa. They belted them to the truck's rack and drove the short distance to The Cove. They got there early enough to get a parking spot on the street along the fence and before the rental shop across the street opened and started sending over the hordes of tourists.

They paddled all the way to Kamaʻole Beach One, but the wind picked up, and they had a workout on the return trip. After the boards were reloaded, Kekoa said, "Let's go to Three's for breakfast. You deserve a break from being the regular morning cook."

"Chef, thank you very much."

"Oh, apologies—morning chef."

"What time do we have to be there?" asked Kekoa, as they waited for the server to bring their food.

"The party is scheduled from one to four, and they hope to have everyone out by six. I want to be there by twelve to help set up."

"What did you get for the baby?"

"A size 18-month party dress for her to grow into. Why are you smiling?"

"It's nothing," he said, recalling his first day at MPD. "You were saying?"

"As you might guess, I'm not the only tall Reynolds, so my brother's kids get big fast. And this neat bathtub toy. It's five different stackable buckets with different animal faces on each one. So, stacking them on the floor helps develop a baby's motor skills. When you fill them with water, the water sprinkles differently from three of them."

"Why not five different ways?"

"How would I know? It's a kid's toy! Stop being so logical.

"Oh, and Babe, I signed the card from both of us. You don't mind, do you?"

"No, that's fine." *Is that like telling her family we're a couple?*

LIA SHOWERED FIRST, so that her hair would have time to dry. Kekoa went out to his car to get his clean clothes before he showered and shaved. He brushed his teeth again, deodorized, and patted his face with shaving balm.

When he went into the bedroom, Lia had already put on a sleeveless, moderately low cut, yellow sun dress with spaghetti straps that fit her like a glove until it dropped down past her hips. *Well, if you've got it, flaunt it.*

"Wow! What a beautiful dress, sweetie. Your tan really looks good with that bright yellow."

"Thank you, Kekoa. I just bought it for this party. I'm glad you like it. I bought something for you, too. I know you weren't planning on staying here so long and you didn't bring lots of clothes, so I bought you a new shirt. I got it at Crazy Shirts in Wailea, so we can take it back if you don't like it." She reached into the closet and removed a hanger holding a classy-looking polo shirt. "I hung it up so a few wrinkles would fall out. If you like it, I'll take the tags off."

He could tell she was waiting for his response, which came quickly. "I love it, Lia! Great floral pattern, and the green adds just the right amount of color to the browns and beige." He saw that she was beaming that he was pleased. "Oh, and I notice it contrasts well with your yellow dress, but you probably hadn't noticed that."

She gave him side eyes and smirked.

"Oh, good. I'm glad you like it." She snipped off the tags with a small scissors and handed it back. "Try it on."

He pulled it over his head, stuck his arms in the holes, and pulled it down. "Perfect fit. What do you think?"

"I like it; it looks good on you."

He was appreciating her cleavage while she buckled the straps on new sandals. "We'll take my car, okay? I think the fruit bowls will travel better on the back-seat floor."

"All right. Let's go next door and get them." When they passed the chicken coop, she said, "Look, the mango rinds are all picked clean already."

When they got turned onto South Kīhei Road, Lia asked, "Do you know where Ace Hardware is?"

"I think so. It's been a while. Behind the post office, right?"

"Yes. We need to stop at the Maui Hub truck behind the hardware store and pick up our fresh produce. The truck's here only between noon and two."

"Is that why there's a cooler with an ice pack in the back seat?"

"Good deduction, detective."

"I thought you wanted to be to your brother's by twelve."

"So? We'll be a little late but still be early."

Kekoa laughed. *How does one argue with Venusian logic?*

* * *

CHAPTER 34

LIA HAD SAID the family home wasn't near the top of the housing development, but it was darn close in Kekoa's estimation. The view across the valley was breathtaking. He could see the harbor, the airport, ever-expanding Kahului, and all the varied crops growing on the vast agricultural acreage.

"You coming?" Lia teased, already out of the car and holding the two presents, one in child-birthday wrapping and the other in a gift bag.

"Be right there. Just taking in this view." He reached in for one of the large bowls and came around the car to join her.

A large man, both in height and breadth, who looked vaguely familiar to Kekoa, came out of the house with a wide smile. "Hey, sis!" he shouted.

"Aloha awakea, bra!" she responded before they exchanged hugs and honis. "Honey, this is my brother, Jason Kahiau. Jason, this is Kekoa."

Kekoa juggled the bowl into the crook of his left arm to shake hands. While they were looking at each other, he saw a look of curiosity on her brother's face. He had already noticed Jason had tattoos around both wrists and an ala niho down the length of his left leg. Kekoa guessed him to be around six-three and 225 pounds; the guy was buff.

"Jason, there's another bowl on the floor in the back. Would you please get it?"

Jason caught up to them before they got to the front door and held it open for them. "Kekoa, after you set that down, would you please park in the driveway? Bumper lock my wife's car, and we may have room for one more behind you."

"Will do. Lia said to leave the driveway open in case you got called out."

"Not today. Peggy would kill me. Unless I see the county building on fire," his eyes swept the panoramic view of the valley, "I think we're all good." Kekoa interpreted the "we" to be his firefighter brothers likely to be in attendance.

Inside, Kekoa saw a lovely woman admiring Lia's new dress. She wasn't "old" but older than Lia. The two favored each other, so it was obviously her mother. It was easy to see where her children had gotten their stature *and* their looks.

"Sweetheart, this is my mom, Cynthia Kamalani Reynolds. Mom, Justin Kekoa Opio."

They exchanged a brief hug and cheek busses in the Hawaiian style.

"'Cindy' will do just fine," she said. "It's so nice to meet you, Kekoa, after hearing so much about you."

Kekoa cut a quick glance at Lia that she returned with a half-shrug and a crooked grin.

"The pleasure is all mine, ma'am."

Lia took Kekoa's hand and turned him to the side a bit. "This is my sister-in-law—"

"Peggy Kelly!" he exclaimed.

She smiled back broadly, "Justin Opio!"

Cindy, Jason, and Lia all exchanged curious looks with each other as the pair exchanged honis.

"You haven't changed a bit since tenth grade!"

Peggy patted her hips, "Well, maybe a little after three kids."

Kekoa looked at Lia but said it for everyone's benefit. "We went to St. Anthony's from first grade until my family moved."

"And I graduated from there," she added proudly.

"Did you maintain your perfect attendance?"

"You bet I did! Even got a little pin to prove it," she chuckled.

Jason put a hand on Kekoa's shoulder and turned him. "I knew I recognized you when you got out of the car. We played Junior Division Little League together."

"I thought there was something familiar about you, too. You were tall but way thinner back then."

"Well, you know us firefighters. If we're not polishing our trucks, we're pounding the weights, waiting for the alarm to go off."

The three women were standing there, thoroughly enjoying this repartee.

"You look like you could pull the darn truck if you had to," Kekoa told him, and not facetiously.

"You think you're kidding," said Peggy. "They have competitions to see who can actually do that."

Jason shrugged. "Just friendly little wagers. No one ever budges it more than an inch or two." Everyone laughed.

Lia took his hand. "Come on, Babe. Let me show you where I grew up."

The other three Reynolds all exchanged knowing, but approving, looks as the young couple left.

The ranch-style house had a wide, open floor plan. All tiled with accent rugs fashionably placed. The kitchen, formal dining area, family room, and living room all flowed into each other, interrupted by only one, short load-bearing wall and two pillars. Lia was leading him to a hallway when they approached a bookshelf in a wall. A triangular wooden display box was resting on one shelf that contained a folded American flag. A brass plaque read: MSGT TIMOTHY K. REYNOLDS above the dates of his birth and death.

Kekoa stopped, forcing Lia to stop while she still held his hand. His eyes reached into hers. "I *knew* your dad." She watched him looking at the flag, obviously recalling memories. "He used to coach one of our Little League teams." He looked back at her, "He was a great guy, and a good coach."

"Thank you. I thought so, too. I'm glad you knew him."

"This is Josh's room," she said, indicating the first one on the right; a peek inside made it obvious it was a boy's room. "My brother's and Peggy's is at the end of the hall, and this one," she said, "is the girls' room, which used to be mine."

She very quietly opened the door far enough to stick his head in. A small bed with a Pretty Pony spread on it was against the far wall, and closest to the door was the crib, where the baby was sleeping. Back out in the hall, she said, "We can come back later, and I'll tell you more about my time here."

"Like how you used to sneak out in high school?"

"Oh, that's just for starters," she laughed.

Kekoa followed Lia back down the hall, where she crossed the family room to a large sliding glass door and pulled it open. A young boy and a younger girl wearing arm floaties were playing some kind of game in the pool.

"They're being quiet right now because they know they'll get in trouble if they wake the baby," Lia told him. No sooner had she said it than the boy screamed, "Auntie Lia!" He popped out of the water so fast it reminded Kekoa of a seal or a penguin.

Lia snatched a fluffy beach towel off the chaise lounge and caught the boy in it before he got her dress wet. She hugged him and gave him several noisy kisses on his face that he quickly wiped off while she continued patting him dry.

"Lawakua, this is auntie's friend, Kekoa."

The boy held out his hand to shake and said, "Aloha, uncle," the Hawaiian term of respect for any older male. Kekoa looked at Lia—they both knew what the other was thinking about the title—and shook the boy's hand, noticing the boy looking him in the face as he did. "Nice to meet you, Lawakua."

Not far behind came a small girl. She was not as fast out of the water as her brother and had to use the steps. Kekoa saw that both children had inherited their mother's auburn hair.

"Aloha, Auntie Lia," came the little-girl voice.

She didn't try running into Lia, who said, "Let's take off your floaties," and did so; then she wrapped another towel around the child.

"Sweetheart, this is my niece, Jada Nāmaka. Nāmaka, this is auntie's special friend, Kekoa.

The child was standing at Kekoa's feet and craned her head back to look up at him. "Aloha, uncle."

"Aloha nō, Nāmaka," he beamed back.

"Pat them off so they're at least not dripping when they go in the house," instructed Lia.

He guessed his patting was somehow tickling the little girl, or she thought so, at least, and started squirming and squealing with giggles. Lia looked at him, appreciating his tenderness with her niece, but also shaking her head. "Peggy will kill you if you wake up that baby. All she needs is a cranky kid at her own party."

"Me? It was your idea to get them out of the pool," which wasn't true, but two could play the blame game.

As directed, Kekoa took the towels back out onto the lānai to drape over the deck chairs to dry while Lia herded the children toward the kitchen. When he came back in, the women, including the female half of another couple who had arrived, were busy arranging things for the potluck. The kids were sitting at a small play table with matching small chairs, eating their lunch. Jason was handing the newcomer a blue-and-white can of beer and held one up in Kekoa's direction, with a raise of his chin.

"Sure. Mahalo," he said, accepting the chilly can of Blue Swell.

"Oh, yeah, I nearly forgot. Guys, can you put these sleeves on your cans? Keeps the floors from getting slippery."

Kekoa accepted one and examined the lettering before sliding it on the can. "Firefighters have longer hoses." He caught Lia's eye and held it up. She smiled and nodded that she had seen it before. He then remembered that her ex, who he already hated, was likely to be here.

Jason introduced the other fellow as Frank Seaman. *Shit, I'll bet he's been kidded about that since he was a kid.* "Frank and I work at the same station. He's an engineer, which means he drives and maintains the working parts on the engine."

Kekoa tipped back his brew and said, "Oh yeah? How much water does your truck carry?"

"There're bigger ones, but ours carries 750 gallons and can put out 1500 gallons a minute."

Kekoa thought about that for a second, shook his head, and said, "But then you're empty in thirty seconds."

The firefighters looked at each other and laughed. "That's only if we're pumping at full pressure. When we pull up, I immediately start turning on all the pumping equipment, watching the pressure come up. Jason and other guys are pulling the attack line—the hose—off the back of the truck to pull it to the fire, and other guys are pulling out a larger, supply line and getting it to the nearest hydrant—"

"Ahh, so, as fast as the water is going out, more is coming in." Jason and Frank nodded, smiling. Two more obvious firefighters arrived and went straight to the refrigerator and got their own beers and sleeves.

"Kekoa's a cop," Jason told them, "So, no surprise he's a little slow."

"Actually, I'm a deputy sheriff over here on a temporary detail, but I'm glad to see the police-fire rivalry is as healthy here as it is in California."

"You're from California?" said a guy introduced as Richard, not "Rick" or "Dick." "You look Hawaiian."

"Thank you," chuckled Kekoa. "I *am* Hawaiian. My dad's in the Navy and moved us there about eight years ago for his new duty station."

Peggy came in from the dining area. "If you guys aren't going to help, would you please go out on the lānai?"

"What do you need done, baby?" asked Jason.

"I thought you were going to have one ice chest for the beer and another for the water and soda."

"Out there getting frosty right now, beautiful," he replied as he followed the rest of them, who had already anticipated the order.

"And you're all on lifeguard duty," she shouted after them.

Nearly everyone arriving had toddlers or grade-school-aged kids with them, who, as soon as they had been showed off in their party clothes, were given permission to change into their swimming suits. The pool was quickly a frothy sea of giggling, splashing, yelling kids.

Kekoa made him as soon as he came out onto the lānai. And faster than the ball in a Major League triple play, the guy made eye contact with Lia. Kekoa looked at Lia, who looked back at him. The guy followed Lia's gaze and made eye contact with Kekoa. *So now you know she's here with me, asshole.*

Lia dillydallied, helping Nāmaka put on her arm floaties until the ex had moved down the lānai and made his way toward Jason and his other crewmates near the pool. Lia stood up and walked toward him. *Darn, she has nice posture. I have to tell her that. And she looks stunning in that dress.* Kekoa knew everyone, including the ex, was looking at her. When she got there, she took the beer from Kekoa's hand and helped herself to a long swallow; then she handed it back, kissed him on the lips, and walked into the house.

Well, if males piss on trees to mark their territory, I guess that's how women do it—and without one word being spoken.

BEFORE LONG, IT must have seemed everyone who was coming was already there. Peggy signaled Jason, who opened the gas grill and clicked on the fire. Peggy came back with a large box of wieners and a flat plastic Tupperware container piled with pre-formed hamburger patties and a smaller one with sausages, and set them on a folding table near the barbeque. Lia followed behind her with a stack of boxes of buns.

Cindy asked her brother, her kids' Uncle Ed, to say the pule to bless the food. In customary fashion, everyone held hands in a large, if somewhat ragged, circle as a short prayer was recited—first, in perfect Hawaiian and then in English asking Ke Akua to bless little Moana, the entire family, all their friends, and the bounty of the ʻāina they were about to enjoy. Kekoa laughed internally: another descendant of Chester Davies the carpenter.

The kids were called out of the pool when the hot dogs and first hamburgers were ready. After they went away for the other side dishes, Jason went right to work on the thicker burgers and bratwurst for the adults. Two other six-foot folding tables under the pergola were laden with all the potluck offerings.

Kekoa tried to help by picking up fallen napkins before they blew into the pool, gathering used paper plates, and collecting the empties. He sorted the plastic bottles and cans into trash cans prepared with liner bags and appropriate signage, though the latter had minimal effect. Every so often, his and Lia's eyes would meet, and they would both smile.

He finally decided to get a burger and was second in line at the grill. When he realized he was getting buzzed after his third beer, he switched to water and was glad he had when Cindy came up behind him. He expected her to ask if he was having a good time or other friendly conversation starter, but getting right to the point seemed to be an attribute of the Reynolds family, and there was little doubt where Lia had acquired it.

"She's quite a girl, isn't she?"

"A 10 in my book, if you don't mind my saying so," replied Kekoa.

"Not at all," she said.

Kekoa wasn't sure where this conversation was going, so he tried to change the subject. "Did Lia tell you I knew your husband? He was one of the coaches when I was in Little League."

"No, but Kahiau thought you might remember him."

"He was a great mentor for teenage boys at a time when a Marine master sergeant is what we often needed. I'm sorry you *all* lost him."

Cindy signaled her appreciation for those sentiments with her eyes. "I am, too," she said softly.

"I suppose you've met David Sentz?"

Kekoa had covertly asked around and learned that was the name of the asshole who used to be in Lia's life. "No, I haven't, and, from what Lia told me, I don't care to." Anything else he might have said he relayed with the look he sent to Cindy. She smiled, nodded, and walked away.

Kekoa moved up with his plate. "I haven't been able to catch you alone, but do you prefer 'Jason' or 'Kahiau'? I can call you either one."

"Here and the beach and most everywhere else, I prefer 'Kahiau.' You know we're native Hawaiians?"

Kekoa smiled and nodded. "Oh, yes, I do."

Kahiau laughed, knowing where that smile had come from. "Hawaiian names, haole names, and nicknames are too much for our one-dimensional captain, so he insists we all go by the first name in our MFD file."

"Got it."

He saw Kahiau's son within hearing distance and added, "By the way, your boy sure has a nice manly handshake and looked me right in the eye while he did it."

The father gave him a wink. "Mahalo nui for telling me that, Kekoa. I'll have to mention it to him when I get time."

Kahiau slid a thick, sizzling burger topped with grilled onions onto Kekoa's bun and put a fat bratwurst next to it; then he plopped a hot dog bun on top of everything.

"Have one of these, too, before they're gone. One of our guys is a transplant from Milwaukee, and he had them flown in special."

Kekoa headed over to the table where all the other food offerings were displayed. He was pleased to see both bowls of their fruit salad were nearly empty. Peggy was carrying little Jessica Moana, the birthday girl, around for her second tour of the partygoers. Lia snuck up beside him and rubbed a bare arm against his and purred like a cat.

"Cat, hell," he said. "More like a vixen."

"Then I'm your foxy lady."

"Correct on all three, angel: a fox, a lady, *and mine*."

They smiled at each other and kissed. "You know people are starting to notice these PDAs," she told him.

"Let 'em. Once again, I'm proud to be here with the prettiest woman in the place, although I have to say, some of these firefighter wives are pretty hot."

She laughed before giving him a backhand to the chest. They pulled two of the plastic deck chairs together and sat down.

"Did you get to eat?" he asked her between swallows of his burger.

"I did—even some of our fruit salad. Good contribution; everyone liked it, and moms love that kind of stuff for the kids, too."

"This mac salad is pretty good."

"Uh, oh—here comes the cake. I'd better go help."

She stood up and bent over to kiss him again, and he gave her a pat on the bottom as she left.

Peggy held Moana while Kahiau stuck a long, thin taper candle in the sheet cake and lit it. Everyone, including the children, joined in a rousing, if off-key, rendition of "Happy Birthday," once in English and, for those who knew it, once in Hawaiian. When Peggy held the baby over the table and cake, Kekoa saw the sense in the long taper. Moana's practice sessions blowing out matches and candles paid off as she was able to extinguish the flame with one hearty puff, without starting her hair on fire or dragging her party dress through the frosting.

Kekoa watched as Peggy's mom deftly sliced the large sheet cake into almost identical cubes while Lia lifted them with a fork and a spatula onto the paper dessert plates, and another woman stabbed a plastic fork into the top. Moana's high chair had been brought out onto the lānai; a large dish towel was wrapped around her and tied behind her neck, and she was given a tiny piece of cake on the high-chair tray that she was allowed to eat with her hands.

One thing about homes on the valley side of the Mauna Kahālāwai: once the sun got over the summit, the air started cooling quickly, and it got darker faster, due to being in the mountain's shadow.

Then came the gift-openings with the expected *oohs* and *aahs*. As Cindy handed her the presents, Peggy read each card aloud and did the unwrapping. Moana got to play with the colored paper, gift bags, and ribbons. Lia sat nearby with a tablet, Nāmaka snuggled up against her, and kept a list of who gave what for thank-you cards. Kekoa stood nearby, watching Lia, her long dark-blond hair hanging down in front of her left shoulder, a hint of cleavage whenever she had to bend over to put wrapping in a paper Safeway bag, and wondered how he could be so lucky. *Blessed* was more like it.

The party dwindled quickly after that. Keiki who hadn't already been redressed were put back in their clothes. Plastic bags were provided for wet bathing suits. Everyone who wanted some was sent home with a dish of leftovers and one or more pieces of cake.

Kekoa didn't know when Asshole Sentz had made his exit but was just as happy not to have seen him again. Nāmaka had fallen asleep, and Lia laid her down on the chaise lounge for now. After the last of the guests had left, he helped the Reynoldses clean up, straighten up, and sweep the pool deck. Lawakua gathered all the pool toys into a large plastic laundry basket and carried them into the housing around the pump.

As they passed near each other, the boy looked up and asked, "Did you have a good time, uncle?"

"I had a *great* time, Lawakua. It was really nice to meet you and your entire family." The boy beamed and nodded his head. "So did I," he said, before moving on.

It was getting dark. Kekoa was not in a hurry to leave but wondered what Lia's plan was.

"Lia, will you take Nāmaka to the bathroom and then get her in her nightgown? It should be hanging on the back of her bedroom door."

"Happy to." She gently awakened the three-year-old and got her walking down the hall to the bathroom and her bed. It was like dealing with a sleepwalker, but the kaika-mahine understood what was happening and robotically complied with directions.

After Lia had her tucked in, she asked if she wanted to say her prayers. "Maybe not tonight, auntie."

"Okay. How about if I sing a blessing oli over you instead?"

The girl smiled and nodded. "Yes, please."

Lia softly chanted a prayer in Hawaiian to protect the child through the night and kissed her on the cheek. "Door open or closed?"

"Open, 'cuz Mama has to bring Moana in after she washes the cake out of her hair."

"Good night, sweetie."

Lia turned out the overhead light, and a nightlight near the crib came on automatically. When she came out, she saw everyone sitting in the family room and heard the dishwasher running.

Lawakua came out, wearing his Spiderman pajamas, to say goodnight. After his dad kissed him goodnight, Kahiau said, "Uncle told me how impressed he was with your handshake." The boy beamed and gave a quick side-ways glance at Kekoa. "See, I told you real men pay atten-tion to how you shake hands."

He kissed his mother and his aunt, and when he came to Kekoa, he stuck out his hand. Kekoa returned the handshake and then pulled the boy into a hug. "I hope to see you again sometime, Lawakua."

"Me, too," he responded.

"Ma hea nā tūtū?" he asked.

"They both went home," his mother told him.

"Tell them I meant to say goodnight, please" and went down the hall to his bedroom.

Lia looked at Kahiau and Peggy, and asked, "Mama went home without saying goodbye?"

"Nah, she went to the 'ohana to put on her suit."

"She's going for a swim?"

"No, we're going into the hottub. You're going to join us, aren't you?"

Lia looked at Kekoa, who replied, "I don't have a suit."

Before Kahiau could offer to lend him one, Lia said, "Yes, you do. It's in the car. Will you bring mine in, too, please?"

Kekoa looked at her, shook his head, and chuckled. "On my way."

By the time he got back, Peggy had already changed. Kekoa tossed Lia her suit and watched her go into the bathroom. Kahiau motioned him to follow to the master bedroom, where they both changed.

"You surf?"

"Since I was a keiki. I've been out with Lia. She's really good."

"We should do north shore sometime," he said, paused, and went on.

"Kekoa, you seem like a good guy. With our dad gone and me being the big brother, I'm her kahu. Yeah, she's an adult, and Cindy, Peggy, and I can see she loves you without her ever telling us. Sentz really hurt her, and I'd hate to see her go through that again."

"I admire you wanting to protect your sister. All I can tell you is I love her very much, and, wherever this leads us, I would never do anything to hurt her."

Their eyes met in mutual understanding. "Fair enough. Let's go take a soak. I already turned the heaters on."

Peggy and Lia were already in the bubbly water when the guys slid in. Kekoa saw Lia was wearing a black one-piece with a strap over only one shoulder. A few minutes later, Cindy came through a gate in the fence by an overgrown bougainvillea bush he hadn't seen before. She was carrying a wine bottle, sans cork, in one hand. She, also, was wearing a one-piece suit, and, in addition to her height, Kekoa could see where Lia got her figure. The woman had to be in her late forties or early fifties and had three children but was still a knockout. He wondered if she had any suitors.

The quintet shared the bottle of wine, news learned at the party, and funny events that had happened, both adult and keiki. Kekoa was surprised, but then maybe not, given what he had learned of the family today, that there was no gossip or backbiting about any of the guests.

About thirty minutes later, Cindy said she had had enough and said her goodnights, including telling Kekoa how much she enjoyed meeting him. As she walked back toward the gate, Lia signaled Kekoa underwater with her foot.

Lia announced, "We're going to take off, too. Please do *not* get up. I used to live here; I know where the door is. Don't worry—we won't wake up the kids, and I'll lock the door behind us."

Kekoa said, "Peggy, it was great seeing you again after all these years and that you married Lia's brother. Kahiau, great seeing you, too, *again*. Small world. I just hope you're a better firefighter than you were a third baseman."

Everyone laughed, including Kahiau, who sent a splash of water at Kekoa as he rose out of the tub.

Kekoa came out of the master bedroom, and Lia was already waiting. She was holding two foil-wrapped paper plates. "We can get the salad bowls another time, okay?" she whispered.

"Tsth, let them have them." He lifted his chin toward the plates. "Leftovers?"

"Yep. The take-home booty. Enough for a lunch or light meal. That's the nice thing about a potluck—there're always leftovers."

They were driving down the long incline, with the city lights to the left, the airport runway lights blinking in the distance, and the vast, unlit dark of the agricultural land below them.

"How many swimming suits do you have?"

"Ten," replied Lia.

"And you wear them all?"

"Of course. They're all different styles, and it keeps me from getting a tan line on my back."

Kekoa laughed. "Can't argue with logic like that."

"Did you have a good time?" Lia asked.

"I had a great time! Imagine all my connections to your family. What are the odds?"

"You're kanaka maoli. You must believe in hōʻailona."

"Of course, I do." More than once today, he had thought about all the signs and omens. *As if I don't already love her enough!*

They were approaching the stop sign at Honoapiʻilani Highway at the bottom of the hill. He rested his hand on her soft, firm thigh. "That's a killer dress, honey. You were definitely the most stylish one there. You always look like a model, anyway."

"Thank you, sweetheart. I liked it, too. But this 'model' body is pretty new."

"How's that?

"You know how you remembered my brother being tall and skinny. That's the way I was, too. Late bloomer, I guess. Needless to say, I didn't do a lot of dating in high school. Boys didn't want to go out with a girl taller than they were. I didn't have any boobs to speak of until they started growing in tenth grade. A geeky guy on the basketball team did ask me to senior prom. We actually had a nice time. I took a "gap year" after high school and went to Australia to surf, with some money my dad left me. Twelve months later, I had pretty much filled out into what you see today."

"So, I got you at the peak of perfection?" he asked, teasing.

"If you say so."

"I say so." He had slowly slid his hand up her leg until his little finger reached the top. "Hmm, nice underwear."

"I know. You have a problem with that?" she snickered.

"Of course not."

"I did at the party, of course, but I didn't bother putting them back on. They were new, too, but you didn't get to see them."

"Well, I did notice it was a thong when I patted you on the butt."

"You cops don't miss a thing," she teased.

"Situational awareness, lover."

+ + +

CHAPTER 35

AFTER GETTING UP early to go paddle-boarding and being at the party all afternoon into the evening, their earlier talk about making love when they got home was put aside. They just got undressed, washed up, went to bed, and were soon asleep.

Something woke Lia in the night. She didn't know what it was—a dog barking, a tree limb scratching the roof, a loud motorcycle, but she was awake. She looked to see if it had awakened Kekoa. No, he was still sound asleep. She turned her head the other way and saw the time on the clock radio: 2:33.

She snuggled a little closer to Kekoa without touching him. She didn't want to wake him, too, but wanted to feel the warmth of his body. They had only the sheet covering them and the house had cooled during the night.

As she lay there, she thought about the fun time they'd had with her family and friends at the party, how proud she had been to be there with Kekoa, which resurrected buried thoughts about the two years she had wasted with David. That jerk. He wasn't even that good in the sack.

Now she had this strong, beautiful, passionate man lying next to her, whom she loved and felt to the depth of her na'au that he loved her. But it bothered her that he never discussed their relationship continuing past his temporary assignment here. Even if his department let him take the rest of his vacation after the case was over, that was only a couple more weeks. Why didn't he ever talk about what happened next? Where did he see this relationship going? Worse, why was she so afraid of being the one to bring it up?

As if reading her mind, he stirred in his sleep, put an arm across her, slid over the couple of inches between them, and, without coming fully awake, whispered, "I love you," through her hair, into her ear.

✦ ✦ ✦

CHAPTER 36

OPERATOR: 911. What's your emergency?

Caller: My daughter is missing.

Operator: What is your name, sir?

Caller: George Kepa.

Operator: What is your daughter's name?

Caller: Uʻilani Kepa.

Operator: Does she have her own phone?

Caller: She did, but the baby dropped it in the toilet. She's getting a new one for her birthday.

Operator: How old is your daughter?

Caller: "She's only 13 but tall for her age.

Operator: Physical description?

Caller: About 5-5, 109 pounds, brown eyes, and black hair.

Operator: What was she wearing?

Caller: My wife wrote it down for me. Jeans and a Hōkūleʻa T-shirt.

Operator: When was she last seen?

Caller: Sometime this afternoon, maybe around 3.

Operator: Where was that?

Caller: Our house, 55 Fillmore Road, Makawao.

Operator: "Do you know where she went?

Caller: My wife said she went into town to a friend's house.

Operator: Do you know who or where that was?

Caller: No. My wife has been calling all over, trying to find out.

Operator: But you think somewhere in Makawao town?

Caller: Yes. She walked, so it couldn't have been that far.

Operator: Is there a chance she went somewhere with that friend?

Caller: I suppose it's possible, but she's supposed to let us know if she goes somewhere else.

Operator: Of course, but sometimes kids forget. I'll send this information to all our cars. Unfortunately, I cannot initiate a MAILE/AMBER alert without some info about an abductor or suspect vehicle.

Caller: But she knows to be home before dark. She's never stayed out past dark without us knowing where she was.

Operator: Mr. Kepa, is it raining up there right now?

Caller: No! What does that have to do with anything?

Operator: I was thinking, if it was raining, maybe she sought shelter somewhere.

Caller: She would come home soaking wet before staying out after dark. It is really foggy, though.

Operator: Again, the police cars in the area have been sent her description. More cars will be dispatched to Makawao and begin a door-to-door search. One of them will stop by your house to take a photo from any close-up photo of our daughter, maybe like her most recent school picture, and share it with all the other officers. Be sure to call us back, though, if she comes home or you hear from her.

Caller: Yes, yes, we will.

THE FOG WAS so thick Del Kurtz could barely see ten feet in front of the truck, if that far. The old truck didn't have fog lights, and even the low beams were reflecting off the moisture to illuminate a wall of fuzzy gray before bouncing back into his squinting eyes.

"What the . . ." and he had to suddenly brake, swerve, and hit the horn before finishing the question. He pulled over to the shoulder, turned on the emergency flashers, and got out, slowly walking back to see if he had hit the person.

"Oh, shit—I hit a kid," he told himself as he looked at the skinny girl, her long hair askew on her jacket and the ground. Already debating whether to check on her or just jump in the truck and take off, he took a step closer and saw her stir.

"Are you hurt?" he asked the kid as she pulled herself into a sitting position and started brushing the gravel off her clothes.

"No, I just took a tumble when you honked and I jumped out of the way."

"What are you doing out here all alone?"

"My friend Christie Campbell," she began, as if he knew who Christie or the Campbells were, "and I were lying in her hammock in the yard, just talking, and we fell asleep. When her mother called her in for supper, the clouds had already come down the mountain. I'm supposed to be home before dark. I'm in real trouble now."

"Well, let me give you a ride home and make up for scaring you and making you fall down."

"Well, okay. It's not too far."

THAT WAS THE best one yet, thought Del Kurtz as he drove away. He was still jittery from the adrenaline rush, which kind of offset the discomfort of his blue balls.

He couldn't believe how tiny she was. His hands fit all the way around her neck. And the look on her face as he choked the life out of her. *Why are you doing this to me?* her eyes begged. She didn't even fight or struggle. The real struggle had been getting those tight jeans off her after she died. In fact, now that he remembered, he'd gotten only one pants leg completely off.

It quickly became evident that she was a virgin. It was his first, and he hoped he never had another one. She was way too tight to suit him. He finally had to stick three fingers in her to stretch her out a little. Her panties were printed with little flowers; he used them to wipe the bloody cum off his dick. She'd never need them again. The thought made him smile.

+ + +

CHAPTER 37

ANASTASIA THOUGHT DEATH notifications had to be one of the hardest things a cop has to do, maybe after pulling a dead baby from a car wreck. Dispatch said the father had been calling 911 once an hour for more than 24 hours, despite warnings he was tying up an important emergency line and could be prosecuted. She figured Dispatch had given them the right address.

The old, one-story, tin-roofed house, with the obvious addition of bedrooms over the years, was at the end of a long driveway on a gravel road. It was Sunday night, going on ten o'clock, but lights were still on in the house. Even in the dark, a blue plastic tarp could be seen tacked down on the roof. She and Bobby got out of the car and approached the lānai. The air was thick with the smell of pig manure.

"It doesn't get more upcountry than this," said Bobby. When they were at the door, he asked, "You want me to do it?"

"No, I've got it."

An outside light came on before they knocked, the car likely having alerted the residents of their arrival. The door opened, and an older, unshaven man answered.

"Good evening. Are you Mr. Kepa?"

"Yes," he replied in a tone that anticipated the worst.

"I'm Detective Chang, and this is my partner, Detective Ferko. I'm afraid we have bad news. The body of your daughter has been found in a field near Makawao."

The man reached out and grabbed the door frame, as if to keep from collapsing. From farther into the room but out of sight, a female wail went up.

"We identified the body by the clothing description you provided to 911 and her library card in her pocket, but we'll need you or some other family member to come to the Medical Examiner's office in Pukalani tomorrow to make a positive identification. The directions are on this sheet."

Bobby handed the man a photocopy of a standard sheet of paper containing the name and address of the ME, hours of operation, and both the written directions and a map.

"Here's my card if you'd like me to be there when you come, but anyone at the ME's office can assist you. Do you have any questions?"

"Yes! Have you arrested her killer yet?"

"Not yet, but a lot of officers are working on capturing him."

"Good," the man said with emphasis. "My wife and I will be there tomorrow."

"We're sorry for your loss, Mr. Kepa. Goodnight."

When they were back in the car and on the highway, heading downhill, Bobby broke the long silence. "When Mr. Kepa said 'Good' about the killer not being arrested yet, what do you think he was talking about? That we're actively working the case or that the perp is still at large?"

Stays took several seconds mulling the choices over in her mind and replied, "Good question. I don't know. Sure hope he doesn't go off on some vigilante shit."

+ + +

CHAPTER 38

Roger had his badge in his hand and held it up as soon as the door opened. A young woman, lush black hair piled on top of her head and held there with a clip, answered the door. Roger recognized her immediately.

"Good afternoon, Ms. Kanae. I'm Detective Roger Crane from the Maui Police Department. I believe Detective Chang told you someone would be by to show you some photos regarding the incident the other night. Do you mind if we do this indoors?"

Miki'ala pushed the door further open and stood aside. She was wearing shorts and one of her boyfriend's T-shirts as it hung almost to her knees. The front of the shirt read "Does Not Play Well With Others." Roger immediately wondered if the guy was home and if he needed to be extra vigilant.

The home was a small bungalow and not an 'ohana to another residence. Roger followed the woman into what he guessed was the family or living room, based on the couch, two matching chairs, coffee table, and the television.

"Is in here okay?" asked Miki'ala.

"This is perfect." Without waiting to be asked, he sat down on one of the chairs. She sat on the couch. "This shouldn't take too long, but I want you to take all the time you need."

He opened a Manila folder and took out several sheets of paper. "I'm going to show you photographs of five men printed in color on regular paper. The suspect may *or may not* be in the group. I want you to look at each one and tell me if you recognize anyone."

Miki'ala wondered if the cop was nervous or if this was the first time he'd done this, because he kept shuffling the papers, taking the top one and putting it on the bottom, over and over again.

"Don't think you have to pick someone out just because I'm here, because you want to hurry and get this over with, or for any other reason. It's as important that the innocent go free as the guilty be apprehended.

"Are you ready?"

Miki nodded, and he handed her the stack. She moved fairly quickly through the stack, but Roger was watching her face. It rarely failed—he saw the change in her eyes when she made the identification, but, as witnesses often did, she continued looking at each page until the right one came up again. She handed him a single photo.

"This is the guy." Definite but not excited.

"And where do you recognize him from?"

"From the road upcountry when the fucker tried to choke me to death!" she said, vehemently, pulling down the neck of the t-shirt to better display the ugly purple bruising still plainly visible on her neck.

"I'm sorry you had to experience that, but, from what Detective Chang told me about your interview, I'd say you handled the attacker quite well."

"Yeah, I did," she responded proudly.

"Ms. Kanae, there's just one more bookkeeping chore before I leave." He opened up the Manila folder and removed another sheet of paper on which were five smaller versions of the photos in the stack she had just reviewed. He returned the photo she had identified along with a ballpoint pen from his sport coat. "Would you please find the smaller photo of the man you picked out, draw a circle around it, and put your initials in or near the circle."

Miki'ala put the composite on the coffee table and did as he asked; then she handed him back the pen and composite and other photos, which he returned to the folder.

Roger stood up. "Thank you for your time, Ms. Kanae. You've been a big help."

"When do you think you'll catch this guy?"

"No telling. I'd like to say, 'this afternoon,' but we have officers looking for him *and* the truck, around the clock."

"Will I have to go to court and testify?"

There it was. Every witness gets around to it sooner or later.

"If this case goes to trial, it's very likely you will have to testify. I can't emphasize how important *you* are as a witness. You're the only woman—" his mind immediately remembered that kid—"you're the only one he's attacked who lived to tell about it."

"Should I be afraid?" She was going to tell him her boyfriend had a handgun but decided against saying anything.

"At this time, there is nothing to be afraid of. If that changes, we'll notify you immediately, even put you in protective custody, if necessary. It's unlikely the attacker knows where you live.

"But no more pulling over for strangers, okay? If you see anyone following you—or you even only *think* they are, get to a lighted area, and call the 911 dispatcher. Here's my card. If for any reason you cannot reach 911—sometimes they get swamped—call me. That's my cell phone number on the card.

"Thank you again for your assistance, Ms. Kanae."

✦ ✦ ✦

CHAPTER 39

CHIEF MAX KORMAN had told his Public Information Officer to schedule the press conference for 0900, and, at the stroke of nine, he walked out the front doors of the Maui Police Department in uniform and up to the rostrum, which had been placed there earlier. It gave time for the TV stations to mount their mikes on it, next to the department microphone that was hooked into the public-address speakers on the right and left of the plaza.

"Good morning. I'm here this morning to enlist the public's help in finding the killer of three Maui citizens and one out-of-state visitor."

He had had purposely omitted the word "serial" from the opening sentence. He had no teleprompter and only an outline on a three-by-five card of the items he wanted to cover.

"Through the diligent work of Maui PD detectives, we have identified the primary suspect as Delbert John Kurtz, 44, from Oakland, California. He has hazel eyes and brown hair, stands five feet, eight inches, and his last known weight was 160 pounds. He has no prior criminal record but should be considered armed and dangerous. Photographs will be provided to you at the end."

As a courtesy and with the understanding the photos would not be publicized prior to the press conference, digital copies had already been sent to the television stations, so they could put the suspect's image on their screens as the chief spoke. The photo was a composite, including the one from Kurtz's Washington State driver's license and the photo captured by the McDonald's security camera.

"At present, we believe he is still driving a faded-green 1979 Datsun pickup truck with a white camper shell on the back. The truck was stolen just over a week ago and may still have the original license plate—" He read the three-letter-and-three-number combination of the plate. "Photos of the truck and license plate will also be provided following this conference. In addition, Wanted posters will be put up in all areas where people congregate."

Again, digital versions of the photos had been sent to the TV outlets prior to the conference.

A protest had started on the sidewalk outside police headquarters, concurrent with the departmental conference, and was increasing in volume, even competing with the big speakers. They shouted chants and slogans through an electric megaphone and carried signs:

JUSTICE FOR U'ILANI
MPD DOESN'T PROTECT KANAKA KEIKI
FIND THE CHILD KILLER

"I will take a few questions. Yes, Shelley."

"Is there any truth to the rumor, Chief Korman, that the victims had been raped?" asked the local stringer for a Honolulu TV station.

"Yes. Sadly, that is true."

A gasp arose from most of those in attendance.

"Yes, Norene." He pointed to the tall reporter.

"Given the length it has taken your department to get to this point, what kind of time frame do you expect before the suspect is arrested?"

"Initially, we thought we had three different killers. We had three victims: different ethnicities, different occupations, different ages, and in three widespread areas, Lāhaina, Kahului, and Hāna.

"Once we determined it was likely a serial killer, we refocused our investigation, brought in an outside expert, and created a dedicated team of my best investigators. The fact that there is only one certified crime lab in the state, at Honolulu PD, builds in delays of its own. We are very thankful for the assistance HPD has provided so far, but it is only human nature that they will give priority to their own cases before processing evidence from the neighbor islands."

The chief knew that, if the news conference received any television play, it would also be aired in Honolulu County. Let HPD whine, as long as it got a faster turn around on his evidence.

"So as to your question about how soon until we arrest this monster, I can't say, except that we are closer to the end of this case than the beginning. He can't use the airport or the ferry to leave the island, so unless he is going to paddle a canoe or try to swim, he has nowhere to go. With the help of you folks in the news media giving repeated coverage of these photos, we will have the 145,000 residents of Maui helping us find him."

"Chief, please, a follow-up question." The chief signaled her to continue.

"You said, quote, 'Once it was determined it was likely a serial killer,' unquote. What was it that led you to that determination?"

"Excellent question, but unfortunately one I'm not at liberty to comment on at this point.

"Thank you all for coming."

IT WAS LATER that morning when Detective Ferko called across the room to the team's putative detective sergeant. "Stays, I got as much information as I could run down on Mr. Kepa."

"Let's have it."

"He's fifty-nine years old, married to the same woman since twelfth grade, when he dropped out. Five children, four adults, and the dead girl was their late-in-life baby. He's had one DUI conviction and two disorderly conduct arrests that were never prosecuted. All from 30 years ago.

"He hunts, raises, and butchers hogs. The ones he raises are mostly piglets, captured after the mother is killed. He's one of the primary providers for lūʻau hogs to the big resorts as well as backyard pig roasts. He and two of his brothers are registered hunters with DLNR for the axis deer-eradication program. He butchers the deer and gives away venison to anyone who wants it, plus supplies a lot of raw meat to the humane society and various dog-rescue organizations."

"Thanks, Bobby. Good work.

"Remember last night, when you asked me if the victim's father was happy because we're actively working the case or because the killer was still on the loose? Is this what you were afraid of: the dead girl's dad and uncles are professional hunters and undoubtedly well-armed?"

✦ ✦ ✦

CHAPTER 40

DEL KURTZ WAS buying gas for the truck and watching the news on a little TV screen above the pump. He thought he would shit a brick when he saw his picture with his name superimposed underneath it. He quickly scanned the immediate area to see if anyone was watching him. Good, the coast was clear. Then he saw photos of the truck on the TV. He stopped fueling at 25 dollars. It was more than enough and all he wanted to spend right now. *Lucky for me this little truck gets good mileage*, he thought.

He hung up the hose, got in, and was about to drive away when he saw an O'Reillys Auto Store about a half block down the street on the other side of the road. He'd have to chance it that they hadn't seen the news. He drove over there and parked at a dry cleaner next door. Even though he had just counted his money at the Quik Stop, he counted it again. He had more than enough.

A bell rang somewhere when he came in, but he saw only two employees, one stocking shelves and the other ringing up a customer. His cap brim was already pulled low, he had a three-day growth of whiskers, and kept his sunglasses on inside. Del scanned the product list at the end of each aisle and saw what he wanted.

Lucky day! They even had flat olive green. He got two of them and one flat black; then he pretended to look at other products until the other customer left. They had bright colors in a cheaper brand, but he had to get the more expensive Krylon.

"Will that be all, sir?"

"Yes, thank you. No, wait. How much are those O'Reilly ball caps? Mine is getting pretty grungy."

"On sale for three ninety-nine."

"Okay. I'll take one."

"That will be twenty-eight seventy-nine. Would you like a bag?"

"Yes, please," he replied and handed the guy a ten and a twenty, mentally refiguring his remaining cash. "Could you put the cap in a separate bag?"

Back in the truck, he had to find a place to lay low until dark. Well, dusk, anyhow. He'd need *some* light. He decided to go back down Hāna Highway and find some little-used road like ones he had found previously to sleep at night. The amount of underbrush that grew over from the sides was a sign of infrequent traffic. On the way, he'd stop at the public bathroom in the parking lot for all the tourists who crossed the road to go look at those waterfalls. They would give him dirty looks for shaving in the sink, but tourists would never pay attention to his face.

The sheet of stainless steel or whatever metal it was that was supposed to act as a mirror was so scratched up that he could barely see what he was doing. He could never have done this after dark. To make things worse, his cheap BIC razor was dull and kept pulling the whiskers. Every moment he cursed his decision to shave and reminded himself he had to change his appearance. He ended up with a pretty respectable Fu Manchu mustache and a terrible case of razor burn.

Tomorrow, after the truck had its new look, he'd have to find a beach with public showers. It would also give him a chance to rinse out his T-shirts.

LIA RARELY WATCHED the news and then only if it was something interesting happening on Maui or to catch the weather report. She had turned on the small flat-screen mounted on the wall in the bedroom when she got home from work. Kekoa had told her the chief of police was going to give a press conference and guessed it might be on the news. She took off her T-shirt and bra and stepped out of her shorts and underwear. She hadn't spilled a drop all day but swore the shirt smelled like steamed milk and used coffee grounds.

There it was! She fell across the bed to get to the remote on the nightstand and turned up the volume. Once during the chief's remarks, the camera, or a later edit, had cut away to a demonstration on the public sidewalk in front of police headquarters. When that segment ended, she left the TV on to catch the weather, which she would be able to hear from the bathroom.

She washed her face and armpits, and recharged her deodorant.

The 5:30 news was just beginning when she heard Kekoa's key in the lock. He came in carrying his leather shoes and heard Lia shout from the bedroom.

"Come quick, Babe—the chief is going to mention you on the news!"

He came in, put his shoes in the closet, and looked at her sprawled on the bed.

"That's what I like to see when I get home from work—my naked girlfriend on the bed."

"Oh, hush. I was just changing clothes and didn't want you to miss it. I hope they show it again." She got up and pulled on a pair of cutoffs and a tank top. If he had called attention to the fact the tank nicely displayed a portion of the sides of her breasts, she would have put on a tube top or something.

He also changed into shorts and a tank top in time to hear her say, "Shhh, here it is!"

I wasn't saying anything!

They listened to the news coverage again. Kekoa could only imagine the pressure the chief was under. *What else can the team do to nail the killer?*

"Well, didn't you hear him mention you?"

"I didn't hear 'Justin,' 'Kekoa,' or 'Opio' one time."

She gave him a playful swat. "We 'brought in an outside expert!' Who do you think he was talking about?"

"Hard to feel like an expert after all the days without any progress, but we're closing in on him now."

"I felt so sorry for that father at the demonstration. The sign he was carrying made me want to cry. How come you never told me about that case or that the women had all been raped?"

"What would it have accomplished except make you want to cry? I saw that little girl dumped in that field and I wanted to kill whoever did it."

"She was such a pretty girl," Lia said, referring to the two photos on her father's sign. "But the one of her, I guess it was at the morgue—"

"It was. First time I've ever known a relative to take a photo of their loved one on the slab."

"That one looked so stark. Even her brown skin looked a sickly beige."

RACHEL MARTINEZ TURNED on the television before she started taking off her uniform. If traffic wasn't bad—usually some pokey tourist holding up everybody—she could usually make it home in an hour and forty-five minutes. She worked as a ranger at the ʻOʻheo Gulch entrance to Haleakalā National Park. Her route took the Piʻilani Highway across the bottom of Maui, where she could look across the turbulent ʻAlenuihāhā Channel to Hawaiʻi Island. On a clear day, she could see the top of Mauna Kea. Farther west, she could see Kahoʻolawe and little Molokini crater before the highway turned uphill to ʻUlupalakua and Kēōkea, and then gradually descended to Kula and Pukalani.

It wasn't the news that interested her so much as hearing the local weather report. Her ears did perk up, though, when the broadcast switched to a reporter covering a press conference at the police department about that serial killer dominating the news of late. The chief was asking for everyone's cooperation, and she would do her part. She always recorded the news and weather in case she didn't get home in time, so she just backed up the program to where the photos of the suspect and the truck were shown and took pictures of them with her phone.

+ + +

CHAPTER 41

As FAR BACK as she could remember, Rachel Martinez loved the outdoors. Every summer and as many times as she could during the school year, she spent every available hour hiking the hundreds of trails in the Henry Cowell Redwoods State Park and the much larger Wilder Ranch State Park near her home in Santa Cruz, California. She had an innate sense of direction, a gift her father had said was unusual for a girl. For a long time, she thought that made her special until she came to understand the sexist nature of the comment, whether her dad really thought that way or not. Nevertheless, she got so familiar with those two parks that she was able to point tourists in the right direction when they were plainly lost or to provide information, often uninvited, about the native flora and fauna.

For two summers in high school, she had worked for Yellowstone National Park Lodges in "food and beverages," which meant she was part of the kitchen staff. That was fine with her. She got a salary in addition to her room and board, worked with kids her own age from various states and even a few foreign countries, and was able to hike and explore the park when not on the clock.

It was sometime during those formative years that she knew her life's ambition: to become a California park ranger. That was, until senior year, when a federal park ranger showed up in uniform at her school's Career Day.

As big as California was, as majestic as its giant redwoods were, and as many parks as it had throughout the state, it was painfully obvious to anyone who read the papers or listened to the news that the state government had been totally inept for years in its forest management, resulting in the loss of tens of thousands of acres of valuable woodlands and the death of countless animals from forest fires. The lives and homes destroyed were an additional, incalculable loss.

After seeing the female ranger, she pictured herself in one of those uniforms. The ranger wasn't armed during the presentation but said carrying a sidearm was a mandatory part of their uniform. During the question-and-answer period, a boy asked if she ever had to use her weapon on the job. The ranger said she hadn't but also mentioned that, since 1913, more than 400 rangers had been killed in the line of duty, more than any other federal service. She explained that many of the people a ranger met in the course of their duties were also carrying a gun, usually for hunting but also for illegal poaching and protecting their illegal marijuana gardens in the forests.

The factoid did not deter Rachel. She was focused on the many more opportunities as a federal ranger than in the poorly managed California parks, and becoming a federal ranger was her new goal. To increase the odds of getting hired, she went to college and double-majored in Natural Resources Management and also Parks and Outdoor Recreation, graduating with honors in both fields.

Consequently, Rachel wasn't shocked when she got picked in the first round of hires after graduation and was told when to report to Flagstaff, Arizona, for the Park Ranger Law Enforcement Academy Training Program at

Northern Arizona University. Sometime during the basic training program, she had to remind herself what her goal was, because, after four years at the university, many of the required 650 hours of classroom work were repetitive and often not as good as the courses in college.

The drug test, background check, and medical screening were a breeze, as was meeting all the physical-fitness standards. She bet she could have out-hiked any of her male classmates, although she had more trouble getting over the 10-foot wall than they did.

It surprised her a little, and also some of the guys who had been around guns their whole lives, but she outscored many of them on the range. She had never fired a gun in her life prior to the academy, so, maybe she didn't have to break or unlearn any bad habits.

She cried when her parents and younger siblings, two brothers and a sister, drove ten and a half hours—spending the night in Needles, California—to attend her academy graduation. It made the event that much more special to have her dad pin her new badge on her uniform. Her mother was a little troubled seeing her daughter with a handgun on her belt, but her brothers thought she was "cool."

The letdown came the next day, when she learned she had not been hired on as a full-time ranger but rather only for a seasonal position. She would have to do that for two or three seasons before she could be hired full-time. But her foot was in the door, so to speak, and she would be promoted to full-time in due course.

Rachel was elated when she learned her first seasonal post would be America's first national park, Yellowstone! Although the park is larger than Rhode Island and Delaware combined, she had spent two summers there and knew where all the entrances were, most of the roads, and a number of trails. She also had an encyclopedic knowledge of all the animals that lived there and could share that knowledge with the tourists.

Her elation came down several notches when she was told she would be there in the winter.

Tourism was minimal, the bears and some other animals were all hibernating, and the park was buried in snow most of the season. Thank God for the generous uniform allowance to cover all the winter gear that made her feel like an Eskimo. She even had to wear a special holster rig on the outside of her parka across her chest.

She did enjoy touring the white wilderness on a snowmobile, seeing the bison covered in white after a storm, and the brief affair she'd had with one of the other rangers. The snow hadn't even begun to melt when Rachel received the new seasonal assignment starting in June: summer in Everglades National Park!

She realized two pluses right way. She would be able to change to summer wear as soon as she got off the plane, and there would be no break in her employment due to the back-to-back postings. Wolves to crocodiles, snowmobiles to fan boats—and she loved this job. Every day was an adventure. One thing remained the same, however. Tourists in Florida were as devoid of common sense as the ones in Wyoming. *Stupid* was more like it.

How people ever thought wild animals, bears and bison, for example, were just going to pose while your spouse took some photos simply amazed her. She hadn't been in south Florida a week when this conversation took place.

"No, ma'am, I'm not going to shoot the crocodile because it ate your dog. First of all, they are a protected threatened species. Second, you should have known better than to sit on the shore with your unleashed cockapoo with crocodiles so nearby. Yes, they *are* fast. I'm sorry you think I'm a heartless bitch. Of course, you can file a complaint that I refused to shoot a protected crocodile. Here's my card with the address and phone number of park headquarters in Homestead. Enjoy the rest of your vacation, and drive safely."

The sweltering, sweaty, mosquito-infested summer sped by, however. She must have received good performance evaluations—not that she was surprised—because, after her two seasons, she was hired on full-time and would be transferring to Haleakalā National Park on the island of Maui in Hawai'i at the end of September.

+ + +

CHAPTER 42

ANASTASIA HUNG UP her desk phone and addressed the crew.

"Another breakthrough on the Lāhaina killing." Everyone looked up. "Patrol up there questioned a new hooker who knew our victim. Only knew her by 'Misty,' the first name we have, but had Misty's number saved in her phone. He tried it, and it came back as 'no longer in service.'

"The patrol officer is going to email us a report. Roger, please contact the major carriers and find out if it was one of their numbers. When you find the right one, write up a search warrant. If it's no longer in service, it might have been destroyed, or maybe it just has an uncharged battery, but we want to know when it was last used. Also, ask for any alternate numbers she provided when she got the phone. It might be some relative we can make notification to."

"Will do," said Roger.

THE HOG WAS already dead when they got it back to the farm. George Kepa had taken it with one well-placed heart shot. The animal had been hung up by its hind legs, and George slit its throat to drain out any remaining blood.

A radio in the nearby shed was tuned to 93.5, the Hawaiian music station. The volume was set even higher on the police scanner that crackled ever so often with radio traffic between the police dispatcher and squad cars or between the actual police vehicles.

After ten minutes or so, the carcass was raised higher on the block and tackle attached to a stout branch of the old monkeypod tree. George's brother Henry positioned the wheelbarrow under the animal, and the belly was slit open from the breastbone to the tail, expertly cut around the anus, so most of the guts fell into the wheelbarrow, and some splashed onto the ground. Henry shoveled up the remaining offal. It would be pushed down to the pig lot and dumped out for the porkers' next meal. Nothing went to waste.

George rolled up old corrugated cardboard into a tube, lit one end on fire, and, starting at the forelegs and head, proceeded to burn all the hair off the carcass. When he was satisfied most of it had been removed, he and Henry each held a hose in one hand and, as the water flowed out, rubbed the skin with their other hand inside a rubber glove with a bristled palm until all the stubble was removed.

A cloth shroud was wrapped around the carcass, and the two men lifted it into a chest cooler. They agreed the dress weight would be between 100 and 110 pounds. Tomorrow, brother Tommy would deliver it to one of the resorts in Wailea for a lūʻau. Another profitable hunt for the brothers Kepa.

+ + +

CHAPTER 43

"**M**AKE UP YOUR mind, honey. You don't want me to go alone because a serial killer is on the loose, but you want to stay in bed and try to sleep because you had a bad night. Well, I slept fine, thank you, by the way, but I'm not wasting this flat water. Sleeping-in is what you do when you're old."

"Okay, just be careful," he said just before she kissed his cheek and left.

He knew it was no use arguing with her, nor was it fair of him to expect her to stay home because he hadn't slept well. Still, he knew he needed to sleep, and becoming complacent about fatigue, like anything else, meant not being able to go to Condition Red in a heartbeat.

DEL KURTZ FELT like Harry Potter wearing his invisible cloak. Other than maybe recognizing it as a Datsun, no one would think it was the truck they showed on TV.

He had sprayed the sides of the white camper shell, and a little overlap to the roof as far as he could reach, with the flat, olive-drab paint and used the flat black to paint large, misshapen spots on the truck and camper to give it a military-camouflage appearance. He thought it had been very clever of him to use the paper shopping bags to keep paint off the camper windows.

Last night, he had examined the "Maui Driving Map" he had picked up from a rack of free brochures outside an ABC store. He had decided he wanted to drive to the southwest side of the island and see what it was like. He wondered if there was any significance to all the highways here starting with a "3." He was on Highway 311, but it turned into Highway 31. When he had gone to Hāna, he was on the 36, but, somewhere, it turned into the 360.

It had still been dark when he started out, but the sun was coming up now. Where were all these people going? Most likely to work, but what work was there down this way?

He said, "Oh, shit!" out loud when he saw a sign for POLICE. He looked up and saw it on a hill to his left. No! There it was! Right in front of him! Even before he double-checked the personalized license plate, he saw the MAUI HUB sticker on the tailgate.

Something wasn't right, though. The rising sun was shining in on the driver's side, and he could see the driver's long hair through the rear window. It was blond. That bitch last week had dark hair.

Something else was different, too. In addition to the surfboard that had been on top when he tried to get that dark-haired bitch to stop, a larger board was tied on top, too. He dropped back but kept following from a distance. With the sunrise just approaching, it was probably too dangerous to try anything with the female driver, but he wanted to see where she was going.

He saw her turn right up ahead, and, before he could get there and make the turn, he had lost her. He continued downhill and saw her ahead on the curvy road. She was stopped at a stop sign, with the left directional on. She continued past a resort and some hotels, and then turned into the entrance for two beaches.

He waited at the turn until he saw another car coming up behind him and made the right onto the road to the parking lot. There were only a handful of vehicles but no people there. She had already parked the truck way at the bottom of the lot and was unloading the big board and a long paddle. The girl looked like a swimsuit model, and her two-piece added to the fantasy. She was tall—taller than him, for sure. Her blond hair fell down her back like a cape, all the way to the top of the swimsuit bottom.

He waited until she began walking toward the ocean. The board must not have been very heavy for its size, as she carried it with one hand without any trouble, with the help of what seemed like a handle built into the board. After she descended the path to the beach a ways ahead of him, he mounted a small rise and could see her already entering the water with the board. More people were arriving, and others were walking by on a sidewalk. He decided it was unsafe for him to hang around any longer.

Keeping his head down, he walked quickly but not so fast as to draw attention. He got into the truck, backed out, and took one more look at her truck before turning around and heading back up the mountain, where he felt safer. On the way, he thought about the blonde. No way he could just strangle her. He'd have to incapacitate her first. Could he get close enough to knock her out?

BUSINESS WAS DEAD at the coffee shop that afternoon. The place was spotless; all supplies were stocked. The weekly order for inventory restocking had been sent in. Lia told the part-time girl to take a break while she called Peggy.

Her sister-in-law was the same age as her brother—only a few years older than her. Lia had become friendly with her while she and Kahiau were dating, had been in their wedding party, and was proud to be godmother to Lawakua when he was baptized. The fact was the two women were not just related by marriage but also close friends. Consequently, rarely did a week go by when they didn't talk at least once.

"You busy?" asked Lia when Peggy answered.

"Not really. Just sitting down with my feet up, nursing Moana before I start dinner.

"What about you?"

"The coffee shop is dead, but heaven forbid that someone should try to get in at five minutes to six, finds the doors locked, and burn us on Yelp."

Peggy laughed. "Well, sit down and put *your* feet up."

"Nope, that's another no-no. Only one worker can be sitting down and then only if on break, and I just told the part-timer to take another break."

"Poor you."

"Shut up. Anyway, I just wanted to call and tell you what a great time we had Saturday.

"No one got drunk, no kids drowned, Moana was precious with cake all over her face, and David behaved himself, which surprised me."

"I told Kahiau that if he was going to invite him—and I knew it would hard not to when all the rest of his house was invited—he'd better make sure David understood he had to stay away from you and any guest you came with."

"Oh, so *you're* the reason! When I warned Kekoa about my ex likely being there, his first words were, 'Am I going to have to fight him?'"

They both laughed, and Peggy added, "Yeah, that would have gone over real well, especially with all the kids there.

"So, you're in love with him . . ."

"You could tell?"

"I think it was pretty obvious to anyone who knows you, including your mom.

"And you're sleeping with him . . ."

"Ha! Can you blame me?"

"He's a handsome guy, and it looks like he stays in shape—"

"And he's kind, and gentle, and passionate . . ."

"Yeah, yeah, yeah. I already acknowledged you love him. Does he love *you*?"

"Yes. He does. Not just by saying he does but by how he treats me. My God, what did I ever see in that stupid David?"

"I'm happy for you, for you both. Let me know when he takes it to the next level."

"The next level?"

"When he asks to marry you, silly."

"Oh, yeah."

"Okay, Moana's asleep and just unplugged. Time to start dinner."

✦ ✦ ✦

CHAPTER 44

Park RANGER RACHEL Martinez was heading home in her duty vehicle, a 2021 Chevrolet Tahoe, eyeballing any vehicle that passed her as she headed north on the Kula Highway; she was also watching all the pickups coming toward her. MPD had asked for everyone to help, and she was happy to contribute.

She knew the '79 Datsun pickup from when she was a kid, and it was hard to mistake its size or shape for anything else. Faded green with a white camper was what the police had announced and shown in the photo she had in her phone. She knew not to be complacent, however. Crooks dyed their hair, grew beards or mustaches, or shaved them off. The killer could just as easily have removed and dumped the camper shell.

She was thinking of the cute EMT she had accompanied up the Pipiwai Trail today to help the foolish tourist who tried hiking that muddy incline in slippers. If the ankle wasn't broken, it was severely sprained and twice its normal size by the time she and the EMTs got to the victim. It sure seemed the flirting between them was a two-way thing. His name was on her report; she may have to follow up on that.

"There it is!" she screamed to herself. Coming at her in the opposite lane! That had to be it. The guy had painted it olive drab with a camouflage pattern, but, despite his attempt to muddy up the license tag she spied enough of the digits to know it was him. The dummy hadn't even switched plates.

If he even saw her, he probably thought anyone in the white SUV with the "Park Ranger" decal along the sides wouldn't be interested in him. As soon as traffic was clear, she made a U-turn near Kula Country Farms and started following him about five cars back. She pushed the transmit button on her radio, called her dispatcher, and told him to contact Maui PD that she had the truck from their serial-killer case in sight and was following and to send cover units *now.*

Damn, he must have spotted me. He was picking up speed, and she didn't want to lose him. She activated her overhead lights and siren and started passing other cars as they pulled over to yield. Without slowing down or signaling the turn, the driver turned left in front of an oncoming car and barely missed being hit. Rachel made a quick look to get street signs and keyed her mike.

"NPS unit 2722 in pursuit of a 1979 olive-green Datsun pickup with black camouflage marking. Same license tag as the one in the MPD APB. Now heading south on Kekaulike Highway at a high rate of speed."

The dispatcher responded, "10-4, 2722, information passed on. Switch to channel 12, and you can talk directly to MPD Dispatch."

IT HAD BEEN a good day in the field for the Kepa brothers. Three axis deer killed before noon that had been collected and brought back to the farm for butchering. The animals had been gutted in the field and the offal left for the birds, wild hogs, insects and any other carrion eater.

One by one, the carcasses had been hung up and the coats peeled off and salted for later sale. Little did the brothers know, when they signed up for the deer-eradication program, that there was such a big demand for the unique spotted hides of the axis. The meat, they processed and gave away; the hides and horns, they sold.

They had two stainless-steel tables; while two brothers cut the meat from the skeleton, the third put the meat in clear plastic bags, weighed and marked the bags, and put them in their farm's small meat cooler. Tom had just come out of the cooler when he heard their police scanner. He stopped, listened, and looked at his brothers, who had heard it, too.

"Let's go!" shouted George.

LIEUTENANT DAYRIT PUSHED open the door to the homicide room but didn't even enter. Crane and Ferko looked up.

"Where's Chang and Opio?"

"Went up to the ME's office in Pukalani to pick up the semen samples from the last vic."

"Well, mount up. A park ranger has spotted our guy upcountry. All available units in the area are responding. Reach out to the other two on your way there. If anyone gets him in custody before you get there, I don't want any gung-ho cop taking out some street justice on him or anyone questioning him until we have him down here. Make sure everything is by the book, so nothing gets thrown out in court."

"You coming, LT?"

"Hell, no. That's why I'm the lieutenant. Call me if you can't handle it." He turned and walked out.

Anastasia and Kekoa were already listening to the radio broadcasts when Ferko called Kekoa on his cell phone.

"Yeah, thanks. We heard and are already heading uphill with lights and siren."

"NPS 2722, SUSPECT vehicle is slowing. He's turning right. Stand by for street name."

Pause. "Heading mauka on Waipoli Rd."

Multiple MPD units reported they were en route, gave their current location, and estimated time. The road was a narrow, black-topped surface with hardly room for two vehicles to pass each other without each needing to have its outside tires off the roadway.

"Passing O'o Farm," the ranger announced into her mike.

"Passing Lavender Farm."

"Passing some skydiving place."

GEORGE KEPA HAD a police scanner in his truck that plugged into the cigarette lighter, so he and his brothers knew exactly where the chase was heading and were quickly closing the gap.

HER VOICE STILL calm, Ranger Martinez keyed her mike again. "NPS 2722, suspect is going to crash. The truck is trying to make a hairpin turn on two wheels. There he goes. Suspect vehicle is over on his side. I'm maybe a mile mauka of that airplane place."

✦ ✦ ✦

CHAPTER 45

RACHEL SLOWLY APPROACHED the Datsun with her gun drawn as the dust settled. The engine was running, smoke was coming from under the hood, and she could smell gasoline. The gas cap was on the passenger side, so it wasn't leaking from there. She eased around the front of the crippled truck to assess the condition of the driver without exposing herself to gunfire. The word was he was armed and dangerous, but she hadn't heard anything about a firearm.

She came around the exposed engine block, using it for cover, and could see the suspect leaning against the driver's door. Was he unconscious, simply dazed, or playing possum? The engine was still running and smoking. The odor of gasoline seemed stronger. She didn't want to be anywhere near this wreck if it blew up, but neither did she want this guy to end up a crispy critter. She returned to her car to retrieve a plastic bottle of water and stuck it in her belt.

Because the truck had rolled into a drainage ditch with the top of the camper resting against the dirt bank, she was able to step off of the ground onto the side of the camper without trouble. She eased her way forward, the aluminum shell bending under her weight, and took a quick look in the passenger-side window. The driver was still inert. Switching her pistol to her left hand, she pulled open the passenger door, bit the bottle cap and unscrewed it, and poured water on the driver's face. The driver came to, stunned and disoriented.

"Look up here, asshole."

Del Kurtz looked around for the disembodied voice and finally found its source above and behind him.

"I'm Ranger Martinez. I have a gun pointed at your head. If you make one sudden move or come up with any weapon, I'll put a bullet in your ear. Do you understand?"

"Uh, huh."

"Slowly stand up, with your feet on your door."

It took him several seconds to understand what she was saying and orient his brain to sitting sideways in a tipped-over truck. He finally manuevered his legs from behind the steering column, put his feet against the door, and pushed so his body slid up against the seat back.

"That's the way. Now pull yourself out of there. Maybe put one foot on the steering wheel. I'm taking a few steps back but will be aimed at your head the entire time."

Kurtz finally got enough of his body pulled out to counterbalance his weight and slid over the roof of the cab into the red dirt. He seemed dizzy and disoriented, and leaned on the truck roof for support. The ranger stepped off the side of the camper into the dirt bank.

"Can I have some of that water?"

Rachel pulled her pistol back to her hip and extended the still-uncapped bottle with her left hand. Kurtz reached for the bottle, but, just before he took the bottle, his hand shot out and grabbed the ranger by the wrist, pulling her toward him. She fired, hitting him in the abdomen just above the left hip. They fell into the dirt, rolling around, she trying to retain her weapon and he trying to take it. If she couldn't maintain possession, she could at least deny him any live rounds and pulled the trigger twice, sending bullets into the soft dirt, before he levered the gun upwards, forcing her finger out of the trigger guard.

Ranger Martinez had always been a "big girl" and the 160 pounds of her 5–6 frame seemed an equal match for his skinny body, maybe 150 pounds, and only an inch or so taller than her. But as they wrestled, she had rolled down between the bank and camper roof, and was trapped there, with him on top. He finally obtained control of the weapon and, without a moment's compunction, shot her and ran off.

Damn, that hurt. Gut shot was all she could think of as she pressed down both hands on the bleeding wound just below her body armor. She heard her SUV starting and turning around.

I am not going to die today. She remembered her academy training: stay in the fight, don't give up. *I may be wounded, but I* am *alive. Fuck him! I'm not going to be one of those rangers who dies in the line of duty! He may have my weapon, but he is not going to win.*

She raised a bloody hand to the mike that was still, surprisingly, attached to the top of her uniform shirt and depressed the key. She was glad she was on an open channel with Maui PD.

"NPS2227. Shots fired, officer down, urgent assistance requested. Waipoli Road a mile past that airplane place. Suspect has my pistol and took my Park Service Tahoe."

That about wore me out. She was starting to feel woozy and was afraid she was going into shock. Both hands, one atop the other, were on the open wound. *At least the blood's not squirting out.* She remembered something from the academy about the abdominal aorta running down the middle of the guts and guessed the asshole had missed that. *Have to stay awake, can't doze off,* she kept telling herself.

THE SIREN HAD been turned off, but Del Kurtz couldn't figure out how to turn off the flashing lights on the roof. Well, maybe it would help him get out of here to someplace he could ditch this car. He had a gun now. Maybe he could carjack someone until he found a place to hole up.

✦ ✦ ✦

CHAPTER 46

THE KEPA BROTHERS had heard the broadcast from the wounded officer and knew exactly where she was and from where the killer was coming. All three were experienced hunters and knew the rules of firearm safety as well as they knew their own names. Rule 4: Know your target and what's beyond. The checked their position. No homes or businesses in the immediate vicinity behind or in front of them, which was no guarantee—unimpeded, bullets could travel a mile or more—but the best they could do.

After a quick discussion, George turned his pickup sideways across the narrow road and took a position behind the engine, intending to use the hood for his shooting platform. Henry and Tom proned out in the drainage ditch on either side of the road.

They knew where the guy was coming from. They shouldn't have to wait long.

ANASTASIA AND KEKOA saw the pickup truck blocking the road. But Kekoa was bewildered when she floored it toward the truck. It was too late to change whatever she was planning, which he hoped didn't include broadsiding the pickup. Suddenly, she swerved around the truck, going up the embankment.

"Stays! Watch out! There's a guy lying in the drainage ditch!"

She moved a little to the outside, and the guy rolled toward the pickup at the last moment.

She pulled the unmarked police car, flashing lights still blinking behind the grill, in front of the pickup and skidded to a stop.

"That's the teenage victim's father and uncles," she told him. Turning to George Kepa and his brothers, she shouted, "You all stand down. This is a police operation, and we have control."

The Park Service vehicle came around the curve. The driver was going too fast, and, by the time he realized the road was barricaded, he was about fifty feet away when he stopped.

The detectives were positioned on the passenger side of their car—Kekoa at the front, Stays toward the rear. Both had their pistols drawn and aimed at the driver. Kekoa shouted, "Turn off the engine and step out of the car. If you try to move, we'll shoot out your tires."

Kurtz sat there for several moments. He pulled the gear shift handle into reverse and had barely started to move when he—and the cops—heard the rifle shot and the rapid hiss of the front left tire deflating.

"I'm ordering you men to stand down! You fire again, you *will* be arrested," hollered Detective Chang, furious.

Kekoa had not taken his eyes off the suspect. "Turn off the engine, throw out the keys, and get out of the car," he commanded again.

Kurtz turned off the engine, slowly opened the door, propped the pistol in the door's arm rest, and stepped out. Both detectives' weapons followed him when he began getting out of the car.

"Come around the door with your hands up," ordered Kekoa.

"I've been shot," Kurtz said, holding up a bloody left hand. He put his right hand on the top of the door frame as if using it for support. When his body came out from behind the door his right hand dropped down to retrieve the pistol. Before he could bring it to fire, Kekoa's index finger slipped down and pressed the trigger of his 9mm Glock and double-tapped the killer in center mass. Kurtz dropped to his knees. He would bleed out in a matter of minutes.

He was still holding the ranger's pistol but was pressing the barrel into the pavement, using it to help support himself.

"Drop the weapon," ordered Kekoa, his trigger finger alongside his own handgun, still pointed at the killer. Anastasia had come out from behind their car to better cover Kekoa.

Despite being told to stay back, George Kepa came around the police car, his shotgun hanging in his right hand, and approached the dying man. "Do you remember the little girl you raped and choked to death on a foggy night?"

Kurtz couldn't talk, and blood was already gurgling up his throat, but the slightest look of recognition showed on his face.

"That was my youngest daughter, my heavenly beauty, U'ilani. This is for her." Before either detective could react, the father quickly swung his weapon up, pulled the trigger, and sent an ounce-and-a-half lead slug though the man's heart and into the pavement behind him.

Stays had already changed her aim to Kepa's head, but, without being told, the man opened the breech, ejected the spent shell, and laid the weapon on the road. He then stood up, his hands raised above his head.

"I thought I saw him start to raise his pistol, and I was afraid for my life."

The sound of multiple sirens was getting closer.

TWO MPD UNITS pulled in abreast near the pickup, and the uniformed drivers got out with weapons drawn. Anastasia and Kekoa had already holstered their weapons; both unclipped their badges from their belts and held them up. With their car turned sideways, the patrol officers may not have seen the flashing lights in the rear window.

The Kepas already had their hands in the air before the squad cars stopped. "On the ground with arms and legs spread," ordered one of the patrolmen. The brothers complied. The other officer walked over with his weapon drawn.

Kekoa retrieved the park ranger's semi-automatic pistol, dropped the magazine, and cleared the chamber, reinserting the round in the magazine and placing them on the hood of the Tahoe.

"This guy is lights out. Looks like the serial killer in the APB except for the mustache," said the first cop.

"It's him," confirmed Kekoa.

George Kepa raised his head as high as he could off the pavement. "One of you better get up the road and help that wounded park ranger. She's bleeding out every minute you waste here. Are EMTs coming, too?"

The officers looked at each other, and Anastasia agreed that one of them should go check on the ranger.

"So, what happened here?" asked the remaining officer, who still had his weapon out.

"Holster your weapon," Anastasia told him, her command voice not inviting any argument. "I'm Acting Sergeant Chang. This is an officer-involved shooting. Any statement will be made to IA with a union rep present."

"These men are concerned citizens who stopped to help. Mr. Kepa fired an additional round in self-defense after Detective Opio had already 10-ringed the suspect. They can all be released after you get their statements." She had said it loud enough for the Kepa brothers to hear; if they weren't smart enough to go along, it would be their own fault.

The officer turned up the volume on the voice-activated recorder he kept in a pocket on his tactical carrier vest. "So, who wants to be first to tell me what happened?"

The trio was separated to get individual statements. George explained that he and his brothers were registered hunters with the axis deer-eradication program and were out in the truck when they heard on their scanner the park ranger say she had spotted the truck that was on the news but appeared to have been painted to disguise it. Knowing help might be a long way off, they decided to stay nearby in case she needed assistance. Then they heard her say she had been shot and the shooter had stolen her SUV. They guessed he might come back out the same way he went in, so they were going to stop here to wait for him, but the police arrived at the same time they did.

Almost as soon as the narrative was finished, two more squad cars pulled up. One was a sergeant, who came over, took a look at the three handcuffed men, and said, "Sullivan, give me a sit-rep." The officer gave a quick synopsis, said the detectives weren't talking, patted his recorder, and said he had the other man's statement on tape. "Good job," complimented the sergeant. "Where's Tibayan?"

"Went up to check on the wounded park ranger."

The sergeant signaled the latest two cars to arrive. "Go up this road until you find Tibayan and the park ranger."

+ + +

CHAPTER 47

ANASTASIA AND KEKOA were standing together when the patrol sergeant walked up.

"Good afternoon, Sergeant," said Anastasia, although it was getting on to evening. "Detectives Chang and Opio from the serial-killer homicide unit." Handshakes were exchanged. "This your scene?"

"I guess it is now."

"I can give you a quick briefing. This is an officer-involved shooting. Detective Opio will not be giving a statement today. He'll talk to IA tomorrow with a lawyer present. You can take it from me, though, it was a clean shoot. Officer Sullivan was first on the scene after the shooting and has a good handle on it. Excuse me a moment."

She moved toward her other two partners, who had just arrived.

"Roger and Bobby, please start taking photos before we lose our light. Then go up the road and get some pix up there, too. Who knows when evidence techs will get here?"

The sergeant looked at Kekoa and nodded toward Anastasia. "She your boss?" he whispered.

"Yep. Acting sergeant."

He nodded. "She has a nice style."

Kekoa smiled and nodded. "Champion kick-boxer, too."

A radio crackled. "Sarge, it's Tibayan. The ranger's in pretty bad shape. Gut shot. Medevac is on the way."

"You have flares in your trunk?"

"Yes, sir."

"Find a clear, level place nearby, no overhead wires. As soon as you hear that chopper, light up an LZ for them."

"10–4."

Stays and Kekoa listened to Office Sullivan repeat his earlier narrative to the sergeant. After he walked away, Kekoa said, "Sounds like he has a legit self-defense claim."

"Yeah, isn't that convenient," she said *sotto voce* to Kekoa. She would have to tell Kekoa about her conversation with George Kepa on their way down the mountain. To Bobby, she said, "Would you lay those rifles out on the road and take several photos?"

"Will do."

"Check with the sergeant, but they can probably be released back to the concerned citizens."

Anastasia walked over to where Mr. Kepa was still sitting on the asphalt roadway. "You can stand up." After he did, she gently turned him around and unlocked the cuffs from his wrists.

"Well, Mr. Kepa, we appreciate your assistance capturing the serial killer today. If you wanted personal revenge, it looks like you got it."

He knew that she knew but said, "It doesn't bring my baby back. I would've rather tortured him to death."

Stays returned the handcuffs to Officer Sullivan and asked him to snip the nylon zip ties off the other two. She and Kekoa walked over to the sergeant.

"Sarge, we're going to clear. Thank you for your cooperation and courtesy up here. The stiff is definitely our serial killer. We'll write it up for the county prosecutor, but it was a clean shoot, and no one'll punch holes in Mr. Kepa's self-defense claim . . . and who would want to?"

"All's well that ends well, huh, Sergeant?"

Stays looked him in the face. Seeing no hint of mockery, she smiled, and just accepted the compliment. "Yeah, something like that."

As they turned around, Anastasia asked Kekoa to notify the others. He reached them on their own radio channel. "Hey, guys, when you're finished up there, call it a day. Stays says we'll write it up in the morning. We're heading back."

On the way down the mountain, Stays told him the story about George Kepa and then changed gears and asked, "First time you had to drop a guy?"

"Yeah."

"You didn't have any choice. It's why they let us carry guns."

"Yeah, it's strange. I should be happy I'm alive, and don't get me wrong—I'm glad I am. I just never thought killing a bad guy would make *me* feel weird."

"I'm a friend if you need someone to talk to, plus I was there, but maybe talking to someone who's been in OIS would be good. And I'm sure the department would let you see our shrink if you'll be here that long."

"Thanks, Stays. You're a good partner."

ON THE WAY home, the adrenalin wore off, and Kekoa started shaking with the realization of what he had done, what he had been forced to do. He took the turn to the county animal shelter and stopped on the shoulder. His hands were quivering and his heart felt jittery. They had taught the cadets at the academy about after-effects, both immediate and lingering, of being in an officer-involved shooting, both as the shooter or the target. He had also attended at least two other law-enforcement conferences after coming on the job with instructors who had experienced it firsthand; another was a psychologist who counseled officers after an OIS. It wasn't like TV or the movies, they all said. It wasn't easy for a person, at least one with a proper moral compass, to kill another human. When his body and mind finally calmed down, he started the car and continued home.

IT WAS DARK before Kekoa got to the house.

"You're home late," said Lia after they kissed. "You look tired."

"Worn out, sweetheart. We got the serial killer, though. A National Park Ranger found him, ending up getting shot, and when we blocked his escape route, he got out and came up with a gun at me. I had to shoot him."

She had pushed him into one of the dinette chairs and was kneading his trapezius and deltoids. She wasn't sure what to say.

"Did you kill him?"

"He would have died in another minute, but the father of that teenage girl finished him off."

"So *you* didn't kill him."

"Not technically, I guess, but for the father being there with a shotgun. Well, it saved the taxpayers the expense of a trial and life in prison," he offered with a weak chuckle.

"What about the the ranger? Did he get killed?"

"She. Not sure. They took her to the hospital in a medevac."

"Are you glad it's over?" At the same time she asked, she wondered how soon before he would leave to go back to San Diego.

"Yes, I am. And I'm glad no other defenseless woman or girl will be a victim of that piece of shit. Before I forget, there's a promotion ceremony and a lunch this Friday for Detective Chang, that female officer on our squad—"

"Yeah, I know. Anastasia."

Did he sense something in her tone? Was she jealous? That would be new. "Yeah, her. I'd like you to be there. Can you come? It would just be late morning."

"Probably. Let me talk to my boss," she said without much enthusiasm. "Have you had anything to eat?"

"No, nothing since lunch."

"Can I warm up something for you?"

"Yes, please."

"Okay. You go take a shower while I do."

After a shower, meal, and, if he could stay awake, sex, maybe then they could talk about their future.

"LET'S GO SEE your tūtū this weekend," Lia said as they lay face to face.

"Okay. I'm overdue for a visit and should go see her again before I leave."

There it is, thought Lia. They both knew he was here on only a temporary assignment, but neither of them had broached the subject of his actual departure.

"Are you leaving so soon? I thought you originally came on vacation for a month. You haven't even used two weeks of your vacation."

"I know. But there's something I need to do in San Diego, and I want you to come along. It would be a chance for you to meet my family, too. Can you get off from work?"

"Maybe. I can usually get off, and my tutoring clients are easy to reschedule. How long would I be gone? I have to tell my boss something."

"Could you get off for five days?"

"I suppose. Could we leave on a Friday so I could return on Tuesday, so I wouldn't have to miss hula practice?"

"Sure, we could do that. Plan on a week from tomorrow, then."

"All right," she said, without much enthusiasm.

"I'll call the airlines today and find us seats. Nearly every airline that flies here has a San Diego route."

"Whatever," she said as she rolled over and got out of bed.

"You're getting up already?"

"Yes. I have things I need to do, too," she replied with an edge in her voice.

THE CHILL ENDED before dinner. One thing Kekoa had learned early on about Lia was she didn't waste time or energy staying upset or angry about anything. It was part of her philosophy of living by kapu aloha, a kanaka maoli philosophy of compassion to act with kindness, love, and empathy and to project aloha toward those who are opposed to you or your ideas.

They prepared a light dinner of leftovers and ate at the little dinette with its two chairs. Halfway through the meal, Lia took Kekoa's free hand to get his attention. When their eyes met, she said, "I'm sorry how I acted before. It wasn't very loving, and I *do* love you, Kekoa. I'll be happy to go to San Diego with you and meet your family."

＋ ＋ ＋

Watch for the next book in the series,

The Kahoʻolawe Corpse.

- How and why was a body left at an historic geological formation on an island with no full-time residents?

- Will Kekoa move back to San Diego?

- Will he be asked to assist on another Maui homicide investigation?

- Do Kekoa and Lia have any chance of a future together?